LIGHT SWORN

LIGHT SWORN

DRAGON OF SHADOW AND AIR BOOK ELEVEN

JESS MOUNTIFIELD

DISRUPTIVE IMAGINATION

THE LIGHT SWORN TEAM

Thanks to our JIT Team:

Dorothy Lloyd
Deb Mader
Diane L. Smith

If We've missed anyone, please let us know!

Editor
SkyHunter Editing Team

This book is a work of fiction. All of the characters, organizations, and events portrayed in this novel are either products of the author's imagination or are used fictitiously. Sometimes both.

Copyright © 2021 Jess Mountifield

LMBPN Publishing supports the right to free expression and the value of copyright. The purpose of copyright is to encourage writers and artists to produce the creative works that enrich our culture.

The distribution of this book without permission is a theft of the author's intellectual property. If you would like permission to use material from the book (other than for review purposes), please contact support@lmbpn.com. Thank you for your support of the author's rights.

LMBPN Publishing
PMB 196, 2540 South Maryland Pkwy
Las Vegas, NV 89109

Version 1.00 December 2021
eBook ISBN: 978-1-68500-592-4
Print ISBN: 978-1-68500-593-1

Dedication:

To those who spend their lives rescuing and nurturing the living beings in need who can neither give back or repay such kindness. Such a sacrificial care should be honored more highly.

CHAPTER ONE

The large Texas portal was before me, pulsing. The four large pillars around it stood tall, controlling the area. It was an impressive sight. I found myself standing before it often.

It was a special portal and one I'd been focusing on for the last week or so.

"Here again, Aella?" Minsheng asked as he came up beside me. He held a small device, making it obvious he was there for the same reason I was.

Now and then, there was a spike in activity in the room. We knew it was created by an elf on the other side sending their mind through. Sometimes it was the dark elf I was trying to defeat, but once in a while, it was another elf.

So far, I had connected with her three times. We'd barely spoken the first time, but the second, she had informed me that there were more elves on the other side, and they needed to be rescued.

My conscience hadn't let me leave the Texas site since. If elves needed my help, I would be there for them.

The third time I'd connected with the woman on the other side, she'd let me know more about her circumstances. She was a maid in the dark elf's palace. Now and then, she could get close to the large portal they had built the palace around. It wasn't easy, and she had to replenish her power first.

I was waiting to see if the elf would come back. It was always the same time of day, which made it easier to predict, but sometimes the dark elf showed up instead. I never enjoyed finding him instead of her.

Given that the dark elf had noticed my presence, I'd also been showing up at other times of day, matching the pattern he had held to before we'd opened the Mexican portal. It meant I frequently had to dance away from his connection, but I was willing to touch base now and then and mentally spar.

Whenever I planned to do the latter, I made sure Nuri was nearby. The phoenix was the best of my bonded mythicals at keeping the dark elf from doing anything that hurt us. Today he was out flying and training with the others. He and Roth were able to do a lot of tricks together by combining their elements to create impressive results.

I reached out and mentally connected with the elements not controlled by the pillars, then felt past them until I found the portal. There was a small section still open. It had never fully closed when the great elementals had tried to block off all of the portals in the past.

I wasn't sure how it worked, but it meant that to some degree, elves could reach out to each other and connect across this portal. For the first few minutes, nothing happened. I despaired that I would connect to the female elf today.

Before I gave up, there was a disturbance on the surface of the portal. Minsheng lifted his device as the readings shifted. Something was happening, but it could easily be the dark elf.

I held my ground for a moment longer, half-prepared to flee but hoping I wouldn't need to. In a few more seconds, the mind there had connected with mine. To my relief, it was the warm, gentle mind of the bondslave on the other side.

Henera, she said, the relief in her voice making me wonder if something had gone wrong.

Are you okay?

As okay as I'll ever be. The dark elf has been angry lately. I'm fortunate to avoid most attention, but there's always a chance that the atmosphere will spill over and others will vent their temper in our direction.

I wish I could help.

You cannot aid me right now, and I would not ask even if you could. I'm safe enough. There are many elves who are not, however.

Elves I could help? I asked, taking a step forward to show solidarity but also to lessen the power drain of the connection.

I don't know. They're not very close to the palace, but...

But?

There was silence, but the connection didn't go anywhere. I could feel her fear and apprehension, as emotions often transferred across a connection along with thoughts.

What might I be able to do? Suggest it, and I will figure out if it's doable.

There are other portals, some less well-guarded and some smaller and out of the way. This is the largest and most important, but many of our elves most in need are closer to other portals.

I blinked, wishing the others could hear this conversation. This was incredibly interesting. Over the next few minutes, I got her to describe the portals, trying to figure out where they might be on Earth. It was hard to tell, but she gave me starting points

Do you think you might be able to find any of them? she asked once she'd finished.

It's not something I can promise. I will do my best. There are plenty here who will have some idea of how to find a portal if we can get close.

It wasn't entirely true, but I hoped my words were. There were more portals than we'd found so far, and there were rumors about where some of them might be. No one wanted to find any more. Not until now.

You give us hope, Henera. Our people have waited for the prophecy for so long. I have told others that you've been found. That you have mythicals and allies, and one day, we'll be free once more.

I listened to her words, not sure how to respond. I'd spent these last few years trying to survive against one force or another. At the moment, things were fairly peaceful. The dark elf remained a threat, but he hadn't made another move and had only one portal to reach us through.

If I took the fight to him or snuck elves out from under his nose through another portal, it would be the first time I had made a move ahead of one of his. I would go from defender to attacker.

That was a very different proposition.

You feel hesitant, the woman said, reminding me that our connection also transmitted my feelings.

There's a lot to figure out. I promise I will do my best, I replied, not wanting to destroy the hope she had gained from our conversation. I knew the power of hope.

We will wait for you. I must go now. It feels like he is close.

Before I could ask more questions about what that meant for her, she was gone, the connection broken. I held on for a moment, wondering if I could push through. However, I was aware of the warning in her words. The dark elf wasn't fun to connect with.

I pulled back, panting from the strain of maintaining the connection in a field the pillars blocked. After Zephyr had broken the pillars around the Mexican portal, it had been far easier to connect with the dark elf.

"You were linked for a long time," Minsheng said as the readings on his device went back to normal.

"We need to find another portal," I said, voicing my intention before I stopped myself.

Zephyr appeared in the portal room in human form a moment later.

I heard everything, he said.

Do you disagree? I asked as Minsheng watched us, aware we were having a conversation he couldn't hear.

I don't disagree. We can't let this elf dictate everything. He's trying to make his presence known and get into your head. I don't think he'll give up until we strip him of all support and help.

Even then, he might not.

It depends on how much of a fool he is.

Or how stubborn.

As long as he's not as stubborn as you, we'll be okay.

I grinned; Zephyr was teasing me, although he had a point. If the dark elf was less stubborn than me, it would be useful.

"So, you want to run that by me?" Minsheng asked.

I quickly told him everything, emphasizing the need to find another portal through which to rescue elves.

"You think she's telling the truth?" Minsheng asked.

I wasn't sure how to reply. It hadn't occurred to me that she might be lying, and I didn't want to think about what that might mean.

Did she feel genuine? Zephyr asked.

Yes. Worried that I wouldn't help and afraid of the dark elf.

Then there is a good chance we can trust her.

I nodded, echoing the sentiment to Minsheng.

"Okay. If the two of you believe her, that is good enough for me. There's a lot to be figured out and more to think over before we go looking for another portal. I believe in you and I trust the prophecy, but you still need to act responsibly."

"Or people could die who don't need to?"

"I wouldn't put it so dramatically, but yes."

Minsheng was about to put his device away when it flicked on again and showed the activity of someone else.

I moved back to the portal. There was a chance it was the elf I'd been communicating with again, and I wasn't going to miss the opportunity.

Be careful that it's not him. *You need to keep your emotions level.*

Taking a deep breath, I did as he suggested. I wasn't sure how well I was succeeding, but apprehension filled me. That was an appropriate initial emotion if it was the dark elf.

I reached into the portal area again, which drained me more. I had not been fresh before the first connection. A second would exhaust me.

It didn't take long for me to find the mind reaching out, and when I did, I wished I hadn't.

The powerful dark elf latched onto my mind before I could evade his grip. It felt as if someone were spreading slime over my mind and thoughts, but I couldn't shake it.

Although I fought the invasion, the dark elf pushed harder than expected. I soon felt him inside my mind.

Henera, my dear. What a pleasure. I thought you were avoiding me.

I generally try to.

Yet here you are.

Seems like you missed me.

I like our little chats. You're so...adorable in your hope and belief. Of course, you can't hide that fear from me. You're right to fear me, you know.

And you're a fool not to fear me.

He chuckled as I finally found the strength to push him out of my head. An ache grew in my temples as I severed the connection.

With Zephyr talking to me and Nuri flying in to help, I eventually managed to shake off the dark elf, pulling back physically and mentally as I did.

I panted, lightheaded and not sure I could stand. I leaned into Zephyr as he put an arm around me. After dealing with the dark elf, I always felt like I needed a shower, and my mythicals felt the same way.

I was not sure what gave the dark elf the ability to explore the bonds between me and my mythicals. Thankfully he'd not gotten any farther, but I constantly worried he might.

Minsheng studied his device with a frown.

"What is it?" I asked.

"I'm not sure. I don't have enough data. It's interesting, though. I'll keep studying it. Hope it will give us more information and make it easier for us to combat him."

Grateful for Minsheng and his commitment to helping me face the challenges in front of me, I waited for him to finish.

I needed to write down everything I'd been told and figure out what was worth doing. If I could convince the rest of the leaders in the elven world of the same, maybe we could act in a way that would strengthen us long-term and weaken the dark elf without him knowing.

CHAPTER TWO

It had taken all night and part of the following morning, but I'd eventually managed to put down everything the second elf had told me and list what I wanted to do about it. My mythicals had helped by discussing the memories and experiences Zephyr and Nuri had of fighting the dark elf.

With a plan and more sleep, we were ready to begin telling the people around us. I needed to start with the military, and that meant a trip to see the general.

I found his door open and the commander of the Texas portal sitting at his desk.

"Aella-Faye, my favorite elf. Tell me you have good news. Or action to take. Something for me to think about other than all this paperwork."

"I don't know if I'd call it good news, but it might be a welcome distraction. Although it could also make you do more paperwork."

"Either way, you have me interested. Sit down and tell me what's going on."

I wasn't sure about taking a seat when my mythicals didn't fit into the office. Zephyr came with me and Sen was sitting on my shoulder, but Nuri and Roth were outside. Neither enjoyed small spaces, not to mention the AC unit drying out the air.

I pulled out my notes and went through them. The general sat back and listened until I finished.

"You've got guts, Aella-Faye. I'll give you that. I'll never pretend to understand your kind and their abilities. It strikes me that you're all a lot more powerful than the average soldier, but this seems like a big risk."

"It is," I replied, feeling downhearted. I had hoped the plan we'd come up with would get a favorable response from the general.

The humans of the planet were powerful. I didn't doubt that the US military could overwhelm the entirety of the mythical forces of the world if they wished to, even with my abilities and mythicals.

"Why do you think it's worth it?" the general asked.

"I think the elves we save would join us once they've had a chance to rest. Of course, not all of them will want to fight, but it's still more people to defend the innocent and the planet. Not to mention the intel they might have and what we'll learn rescuing them."

"Those *would* be benefits. But it's still a lot to ask when you haven't found another portal or know if it's defensible."

I bit my lip, expecting the general to refuse.

"Here's what I'll say. If another portal exists on US soil, the President will want us to be aware of it. I will approve a team of human experts to help you find it, and we'll want to help secure it. However, I can't say what will happen after that. It's not likely to be my decision."

After the beginning of our conversation, I was relieved. It was progress enough that I could begin looking for another portal.

I got up and made my way out. Minsheng had gone to one of the labs, and I wanted to let him know what the general had said and get his opinion about where to begin looking for a portal.

Simon, several of the army technicians, Minsheng, and to my surprise, Chris were in the large lab. I paused in the doorway, not willing to interrupt until I saw what they were working with.

It was the device we'd found in the mountain lab, charging gemstones similar to those in my helmet on a bench in the middle of the room.

It was whirring, and Simon appeared to be trying to power it. I came closer and examined the device, trying to figure out how it was working.

My helmet allowed me to charge the gemstones embedded in it, but none of us had been able to charge the crystals we'd found.

As gently as I could, I reached out to feel the elements and figure out what was happening. I could feel the gemstone slowly gaining air energy. Whatever they were doing, it was working.

Simon looked up and smiled at me as I connected with the gemstone. Everyone else finally noticed I was there when Simon switched off whatever was feeding power to the device.

"Looks like you're working on something fun," I said,

intrigued enough to put my reason for being there aside for now.

"Chris finally got this working."

"It's not perfect. There's some energy loss, but it seems to be feeding the gemstones energy."

I nodded, wondering if I should mention that my helmet transferred energy perfectly. While I was usually happy to share information, Chris had betrayed us once. Admittedly, it was the Amcika elves he'd been working for, and now they were allies.

"It would help us if you filled some of the other stones," Minsheng said. "Even if only for a minute or two."

There was no way I could refuse the request. I went to Simon's place, the air elf giving way to me with a smile. I still felt strange when he was around; the man was essentially my creator, but I tried not to think about it and focused on the machine.

"How does it work?" I asked, noticing that the gemstones were connected to pads with a funnel for each one.

Chris quickly explained, telling me to connect my mind to the labeled spikes on the side of the machine.

I did so, feeling the tug as they drew energy from me like the rune-covered tablets did when they were low on power. When Minsheng turned the device back on, the tug grew stronger. I stood and let the transfer happen.

Chris, Minsheng, and Simon pored over devices and stats as I filled four gemstones.

Thankfully I had rested enough the previous day that I had energy and resources for it to take, but it was quickly draining me.

"It's not very efficient yet," Simon said, "Especially with the fire element."

"Heat probably makes a difference," I replied, understanding enough about computers to know that heat and anything complicated didn't go together.

Minsheng's mouth curled on one side, then he nodded.

"I also don't think the transfer from the device to the gemstones is quite right. The pads are letting it leak out."

I switched off the machine and cut my connection, finding that the tug on the rods was similar to when the dark elf was trying to force me to maintain a connection.

I didn't move, and my mind started to whir. I'd always wondered how the dark elf and the woman on the other side of the portal could connect with my mind. My bonds with the mythicals were similar, but I'd had one of those since the beginning. It had always been there, and I didn't feel it needed explaining.

The connection with the elves was another matter. I couldn't talk telepathically with other elves on Earth. Was it as simple as connecting to them the same way I connected to a stone tablet or a gemstone? Or the way they'd connect to me?

I frowned as Chris tried to make the connection between the gemstones and the device more efficient.

Without warning, I reached out to Simon and the elements around him.

He lifted an eyebrow, feeling me invade the space around him and not sure what I was up to.

I didn't explain. Instead, I tried to connect to him.

At first, nothing happened; his mind resisted. However, when he relented, I felt the same connection I had with the elf through the portal. I had to fight not to absorb energy from Simon, and I felt his surprise.

How? he thought.

It's a connection similar to the one with the gemstones, but I'm trying not to drain your energy.

Thanks, I think.

Good to know it works. I'll get out of your head now.

I severed the connection. Simon blinked, and I realized everyone else was staring at us.

"Did you just do what I think you did?" Minsheng asked.

"Yes. Aella connected to me telepathically, using our elemental bond to share thoughts and feelings." Simon grinned. "It's quite the head trip."

"That is...awesome!" Chris exclaimed, eyes wide.

"I believe the correct term is 'mind-blowing,'" Zephyr added with a chuckle.

Everyone laughed at the pun, and it relaxed the atmosphere. I felt carefree again, as I had during early training sessions in which we had explored our abilities just for the heck of it or chilled out with other elementals at the Sanctuary.

When Chris went back to trying to make the device in front of us more efficient, my reason for being there came back to me.

I took a deep breath and glanced at Minsheng.

"I need your help with something. Probably Amcika's help too. And the Sanctuary's."

Minsheng didn't respond but Chris looked up.

"If it's what I think it is, Cherisse is the best one to talk to," Simon replied before anyone else could. "I have a feeling I'm better off staying in this lab and getting these gemstones charged."

"Do we have any more of them? Or a way to make more tablets?" I asked as Minsheng made his way to the door so we could go somewhere private.

"Not yet. The gemstones are a unique design. Dwarf-made, maybe," Simon replied. "And the runes on the stones create the magic, and I don't know anything about those."

Making a mental note to bring that up with the Sanctuary people, I followed Minsheng.

As soon as we were out of earshot of everyone else, I told him what the general had said and about my intention to take a small team and find another portal.

"The organization might be able to help. They've got a team that is good at finding things," he replied.

I thought about my helmet and Tuviel's necklace and didn't doubt it.

"Where's Cherisse?" I asked.

"The Sanctuary. She's trying to get them to help her set up another location for Amcika."

It made sense, and it gave me a destination.

"Okay. I'm going to get my soldiers together and head there asap. Do you want to come too?"

"I wouldn't miss it for anything. Daisy will probably want to join us."

"The more, the merrier," I replied as I went to find the major and figure out who he could spare for the small team the general had mentioned.

Zephyr slipped his hand into mine, but Roth, Nuri, and Sen opted to eat and get some rest. I felt a tug in my stomach as the distance between us grew, but it was lighter than it used to be, and the bonds were stronger since my increase in power. It was becoming a familiar feeling since one of them was almost always away from me.

Within an hour, the major had eight soldiers, including him, ready to leave with us. The organization knew about our quest for a portal, and we had a couple of large vehicles to carry everyone and the equipment lent to us.

Our destination was the Sanctuary. I snuck away to open communications with Ronan to let him know we'd be there before the day was over. I didn't want the border patrol to panic when they saw the vehicles arrive.

With that, Zephyr took dragon form again. Sen sat on Roth's back; the pegasus was wearing a small saddle with handholds and stirrups to grip with her root-like feet. She'd also donned her dragon scale armor.

I had a shirt made of Zephyr's scales too, but it was heavier than I liked, and I had not worn it as much since soldiers had stopped shooting at me. It was in my luggage in the vehicles, however. It was fire-resistant and would protect me against other attacks. Who knew what we were going to need if I was going through a portal to another world?

Of course, we had to find one first, but I was hoping that with the collective minds of the US Army, the Sanctuary, Amcika, and the organization, we had a good chance.

After Zephyr took to the air and I settled on his back, I relaxed. Whatever we faced, we were together. It felt good to be doing something proactive to undermine the dark elf and the unknown threat that had lingered on my mind for weeks.

We were going to rescue as many elves as we could.

CHAPTER THREE

The Sanctuary looked wonderful, the lights from the windows and pathways flickering in the dusk. The only time of day I thought it looked better was first thing in the morning as the rising sun turned it orange and yellow.

Thanks to my warning, Ronan and Dyneira were waiting for us at the border. I bowed low to the centaurs before they could do so. Zephyr, as always, landed at the edge and walked in.

Our vehicles had stopped outside the border as well, and everyone got out. Minsheng hurried closer with a smile on his face. Ronan bowed to us in return.

"Come. A meal is waiting for you. The Sanctuary council and Cherisse are also eager to talk about the quest you mentioned."

I grinned, grateful for how well everyone in the Sanctuary knew us.

We soon sat around low tables, eating and chatting while waiting for the Sanctuary council to join us.

Cherisse was the first to appear, and she had another elf

from Amcika with her—the strong male air elf I'd once knocked out of the sky. He gave me a brief nod, showing no sign of animosity.

"Henera," Cherisse began, "the council tells me you have another scheme I might like."

"So we've been informed, but we know little more than that," Sierrathen said as she appeared behind and smiled at us. A step behind her was Vestan, the male elf on the council. Not long after he came in, a fairy, a gnome, and a treelike creature appeared. When the dwarf Hargraed appeared, we had the full council.

"Thank you," I said as I moved over to give them space to sit.

Once more, I explained about the meetings I'd been having at the Texas portal site, what I'd learned, and what I wanted to do about it.

"That is an interesting discovery," Sierrathen said before anyone else spoke. "Similar to Amcika, we always believed that mythicals had been left behind on our homeworld, but to have it confirmed is another matter. Since they require aid as well, it is obvious what we have to do."

I lifted my eyebrows as Sierrathen paused to glance at the council members. One by one, they gave her brief nods.

"If there are mythicals in distress and we can aid them without substantial danger to the Sanctuary, we must do so. We will help you find one of the hidden portals since you are confident they can be disabled again like the Mexican one."

I couldn't respond. I had expected Cherisse to be eager since rescuing other elves had been her sole reason for opening the Mexican portal, but the Sanctuary had always shied away from conflict and danger. Now the reluctant party was the US military.

"You know I'm in," Cherisse told us when no one else spoke. "I'll do whatever it takes to rescue those elves. Amcika in its entirety will follow me if I command it."

"Hope they will do so willingly, but we've got to find a portal first. And it would be a comfort to know we could shut it again."

"We will help where we can. The Amcika books were brought here, plus everything we wrote down. I'm sure there is information on portal locations of old, even if it isn't complete."

"Thank you," I replied. "I believe the organization is doing something similar. If we can narrow down a location, an alternate portal will be far easier to find."

"I believe I can create a device that will register the energy in the pillars that keep them closed," Minsheng added. "I would appreciate assistance from the dwarves and gnomes here."

"You shall have what you need." Sierrathen nodded. "Now, please excuse us. We are trying to assist in the relocation of Amcika, and also, having so many mythicals in the Sanctuary comes with a great deal of day-to-day maintenance. We must finish our duties and rest. Do the same and know that our best minds will be working to aid you."

I watched the council walk away and noted the look on Cherisse's face as they did. It was clear there was tension, and I hoped it wouldn't get in the way or blow up into another feud. I wasn't sure what to say, however.

Cherisse slowly relaxed, then glanced at me.

"Get some sleep," she said. "You look like crap. I'll get my people working on your problem too."

I nodded as she grabbed a hunk of bread and an apple and walked out of the building, amused and hurt by her opinion of my appearance.

You look amazing, just not as amazing as normal, Zephyr said when I continued to think about it.

Thanks, I guess, I replied, shaking my head in amusement.

It had been a long day, and I'd barely slept the night before. He was probably right, but I didn't want to think about how little sleep I was getting in general. My mind coped better if I kept focused on the task ahead. Right now, that was a rescue mission.

When I awoke the following day, the sun was high in the sky and my mythicals were restless. We were quick to grab food and head toward the large library of the Sanctuary, now more spacious since it had become the home of Amcika's extensive book collection as well.

It was a temporary place for them, but I was glad we had saved them from the mountain and that the dark elves hadn't ruined any of them.

When I walked into the building, my jaw dropped. At least thirty elves were sitting at desks and on the floor. Some were perched atop step ladders along walls, reading.

Sierrathen was there, as was Cherisse, the pair sitting with a thick tome between them and discussing something in hushed tones. Their eyes were locked, and it appeared as if they were arguing.

I hurried closer, hoping to defuse the tension, but they stopped as soon as they noticed me.

"What's up?" I asked, keeping my voice down.

"We might have found something, but it depends on the meaning of a single word," Cherisse replied, her voice anything but neutral.

"An archaic word we can't be sure of. It's dropped—"

"It's a word still used in Amcika. It means doorway."

"But it can also mean portal, a great opening, especially when coupled with these modifiers."

I tried not to worry and instead considered how to get them to calm down.

"Has anyone found anything else?" I asked.

"Not yet," Sierrathen replied.

"They're all looking hard, and some have been here all night," Cherisse added.

"Then why don't you tell me what it says, and we'll see if I think it means what you think it means."

Sierrathen looked at Cherisse, which made me wonder if they would argue about who should read it. Eventually, Cherisse motioned for Sierrathen to go ahead.

"Although the building didn't appear to be as large as usual, it housed one of the portals. It was a minor one and quite small, but it was a portal nonetheless, and that made it special."

"At least, that's roughly what it says, but the word for portal is what we use for doorway."

I frowned. It didn't make sense if it was a doorway, and a portal *was* a doorway.

"Is there a special type of doorway they would describe in that way?" I asked, not wanting to upset Cherisse.

"I don't know of any. While elves do like ornate buildings, it's...unlikely." Sierrathen was calm, but I noticed that she avoided Cherisse's gaze.

I looked at Cherisse, hoping the Amcika elf would either have something to back her theory up with more than what amounted to a regional language difference.

"Given the context, it is likely to mean 'portal,' even if it says 'great doorway,'" Cherisse said, backing down.

Sierrathen relaxed. I was relieved.

"We'll figure out its location so you can go look at it," Sierrathen added.

Grateful I had diffused the tension, I left.

I was helping the soldiers repack the vehicles to head out when Minsheng appeared.

"Good news. The organization thinks they've narrowed it down, and they believe there are a couple of books here that might make it easier to find."

I sighed with relief as Minsheng handed me a printout of a map. Finally, something to work with and a direction to head in. It was a big area, but we could narrow it down.

"I've also got the device I need working, plus some handheld ones Chris managed to build before we left Texas."

With the soldiers and the elves who wanted to join me almost ready, I thought about what else we might need. It wasn't easy to work it all out. Hunting for a portal was a new experience. Still, after an hour, I had the initial group, Ronan, and three more centaurs he'd hand-selected,

Cherisse and several of her elves, as well as several Sanctuary elves, including Gwaelon.

Cherisse and Sierrathen had narrowed down our map further, the description of the area the building was in removing chunks of the map from the list of possibilities.

Finally, we could set off, safe in the knowledge that we had a good target and enough people and equipment that we could probably find the portal within a few days.

It felt strange to fly above the convoy and know we were about to do something very dangerous: make our first attempt to undermine the dark elf's power on his planet.

We flew southwest for only an hour or so before the convoy stopped. Groups fanned out from there, each with a power-sensing device and an area of the map to search.

Rather than teaming up with the elves, humans, and other mythicals, I took a device and my bonded mythicals with me. Zephyr flew us low and slow while I felt for the influence of the pillars that would be around the portal. Sen carried the device to detect the energy.

Sweeping our section was painstaking and exhausting. The constant connection and reconnection to the different elements drained my energy. Since we were in the air, we could fly in broad swathes, and we had soon finished scanning our first sector.

We took a short break before moving on to the next one. I tried not to think about the possibility that everyone had gotten this wrong and we weren't going to find a portal. Maybe we weren't low enough, and time had buried it so deep nothing we had would pick up on it. It wasn't easy to focus.

The longer we searched, the more worried I became. We might be doing this for nothing.

I was thinking we should take a break when Sen's device registered energy and she squealed. Zephyr and Roth circled, helping Sen home in on whatever had caused the device to respond.

I probed below the ground. At first, I was sure Sen had picked up on something like an old orb leading to the Sanctuary. As Zephyr touched down beside Roth and Sen moved closer, I found what we were looking for: the unmistakable presence of pillars within a cavern-like room. It was under the ground on the side of a rocky hill, and it felt as if a lot of the terrain around it was solid rock.

I could make out the outlines of walls, however. Pushing past those, I scanned around to see if I could find an entrance.

I had extended my range so far into the hill that it took me a moment to notice a corridor lined with sand and rock. The tunnel and the entry route had either caved in or had been filled in a long time ago.

However, I mentally followed the wall-lined route to the surface, then scrambled across the rocky surface until I stood by it.

"We can dig in here," I said, beginning to shift the earth before me.

"I'll go get the others," Zephyr replied, flying into the air again as Sen put the device down and rushed forward to pull up rubble with her root-like feet.

Roth and Nuri came forward to help, their hooves and beak helping loosen the dry ground while I moved as much as I could. We made good progress, although Sen and Nuri struggled with big lumps. I got down on my knees and pulled out rocks with my hands.

The soldiers arrived with the off-road vehicles. We'd dug a hole several feet into the side of the mountain, revealing walls that had once formed the halls of a building.

It had lost the entry at some point, and the rocks in the passage had been part of the building. Minsheng pulled me back before we could dig deeper.

"We need to stabilize it and brace it as we go," he said. "I don't want it falling on you or the others."

I nodded, hanging back as the soldiers unpacked and my Shishou got the larger device out. It registered that we'd found another portal and the pillars that protected it.

CHAPTER FOUR

With soldiers bracing walls and adding support beams as we went, I worked my way deeper. Dust, sand, and chips of rock covered my hair and my body. I was getting tired.

Still, I pressed on, although the sun was setting and the sky darkening behind me. Now and then, I paused to reach forward with my mind, checking we were still going in the right direction and feeling for the cavern. The walls didn't run alongside us the entire way. There was an occasional door leading to a room inside the building.

Most of these rooms were as full of rubble and debris as the route we were clearing, but finally, we found a pocket where the walls and the ceiling had held. I'd realized that this had been a large building, going by the fragments of wall and the extent of the corridors.

It wasn't intact anymore, but if I'd had a few more earth elves with me and we had not been here to rescue elven refugees, I'd have wanted to excavate the entire thing and restore it. This was part of elven history, and I could put it back on the map.

The soldiers had called the site in to the general, however, and I had a feeling the government would want to claim it since I owned twelve other buildings across the US and had for some time. Daisy had become my estate manager and put the properties to good use.

Given that Amcika had paid for them, I'd offered them one to build a new home on. They'd gladly accepted, but I got the impression they might not want to use it long-term. The mountain had been their home. Perhaps a building set into a rocky hill would serve instead.

As Cherisse came down the tunnel carrying a tray of water-filled cups, the water not moving, I grinned and reached for one of them.

"What do you think?" I asked after I thanked her and paused.

"It needs a lot of work, but it seems like it might be pretty big."

I saw the light in her eyes and the hint of a grin on her face and knew she was thinking like me. Of course, that meant I couldn't let the US Army take this one and control it. I wasn't sure how they were going to react to us claiming it.

Not to mention someone else might own the land. I would have to find out who did and make sure Cherisse ended up with it, even if I had to sell our other buildings.

"If we have to collapse this to protect the portal again, it won't matter how big it is, however." She frowned as she spoke, betraying more emotion than usual.

"The Sanctuary elves are figuring out how to close them."

"In which case, we'll have a mountain again."

"That's not going to be easy to put back together," I said, surprised but understanding her desire to have her original home back.

The warehouse had become my home, even if I spent very little time there sometimes. It always would be. We weren't going to sell it or otherwise get rid of it. It housed many of the mythicals who had joined me over the years, and it acted as a training base for several more.

After Cherisse headed down a side route, I got back to work. We needed to break through before I ran out of power and had to sleep, or I wouldn't be able to disable the pillars the following day and head through the portal the day after.

Trying not to worry about how the others would react to moving so swiftly, I reached for the next rock and pulled it toward me with my hands and mind. I then loaded it into a cart-like mini-vehicle the soldiers had brought with them.

Once it was full, one of the soldiers could use its controls to move it out of the tunnel remotely, then bring it back for more. I'd lost count of how many times they'd done so, but I appreciated it.

Zephyr worked alongside me, his earth abilities more honed than mine were now, and he soon added a larger boulder that had the cart full again.

While a soldier drove it away, we continued, pulling rubble and rocks in the next section. It was looser and consisted of smaller chunks again for a bit allowing us to make faster progress.

I was pulling at a particular piece of rock near my head when it suddenly gave out. It almost hit me in the face and brought a large amount of dirt and dust with it, making me cough as I inhaled a small cloud.

Pausing a moment, I realized I could see blackness beyond the edge of the hole I had pulled the rock from, and it was crumbling.

It took me a moment to notice it wasn't complete blackness. There was a faint glow coming from inside, although it was barely enough to see anything, and compared to where I stood, it was still very dark.

Within a few more minutes, we had made the gap wide enough to shine a light inside, and then we found it, right in the center of a large room. The portal and the pillars which protected it.

This one looked to be a similar size to the portal in Mexico, but the pillars were larger, and so was the room containing it.

As Zephyr moved more rubble out of the way and the soldiers helped to shore up the last section of the corridor, I slipped through the gap and shone the light across the ceiling.

It was clear that part of the ceiling had given way, but whenever it had entered the range of the pillars, it had been destroyed or flung back out with force. There was a circle of rubble at the edge of the field, showing where everyone needed to be careful.

The most amazing element of the room, however, was the silence. I couldn't hear water dripping anywhere. The air was stale since the rubble had sealed off the room.

I didn't go any farther. I didn't know what might have built up inside, but I was grateful that I had my usual bubble of air around me, a barrier that let me breathe clean air, protecting me in a whole new way.

Minsheng appeared and studied the energy readings. A soldier accompanied him.

"Can you funnel clean air in and the stale air out but keep it away from our faces?" the soldier asked a moment later.

"Probably. Do you want to step to the side and give me some space?"

Minsheng got out of the way. The soldier was reading everything air-based.

I took control of the air inside the dome and the forcefield the pillars created and began cycling it out, carrying it along the floor in a two-foot-high mass as the cool, fresh air from outside rushed in to replace it.

With everyone outside standing back as well, I'd soon flushed out everything.

"Brilliant. Thank you. That would have possibly taken several days if you'd not done that," the soldier said, coming into the room beside me.

I quickly warned everyone how to spot the perimeter of the danger zone, and the soldiers got everything set up to illuminate the interior.

With the added effort of cleaning the air, I was exhausted, and I had no intention of breaking the pillars today. That meant one thing, getting some food and some rest.

Leaving Minsheng to his studies and the soldiers to make the area as safe and secure as they could, I took my mythicals back outside.

Roth had stayed near the surface and worked with a water elf to find a nearby source of water described in the books. A small stream had been redirected over time, but the water elf had put it back in its original bed with the help of an earth elf. I came outside to find the beginnings of a garden.

Roth stood in the water looking majestic, and I beamed. While I was tunneling, the soldiers had erected several tents, setting up some sleeping areas and a communal food hall. They'd also created a perimeter around the whole area and, with the help of the elves, were guarding it.

The major came over to me as soon as everyone noticed I was outside.

"I've spoken to the general. He's impressed we found it so quickly and wanted to offer you his praise for doing so. Also said he'd send out some more men to help secure the area and asked if you'd talk to him once you'd had a chance to get some food and rest."

I sighed, so tired I didn't like the sound of that, but it wasn't the major's fault.

"Don't worry, I don't think the President is going to let him sweep in here and turn it into a smaller base like the Texas portal if we don't need to," the major continued. "I think we're all seeing this as temporary."

"I hope so. In the meantime, do I get to give you orders?" I asked, hoping the question sounded like what it was, me establishing how much say I had in the situation.

"You thought of something that needs to be done?" he asked, not blinking.

"Someone probably owns this land. Can we find out who and contact them?"

"They've already heard about what's happening here

and are apparently on their way over. They instructed us to greet them gently and to give them as little information as we can. I won't deny I was hoping for your presence out here and Zephyr in dragon form in case they didn't take kindly to us being here."

I let out a chuckle at the implied suggestion that facing a dragon would keep someone from being aggressive.

"Then let us get some food, and when needed, Zephyr will take dragon form."

I heard another chuckle from Zephyr as he slipped his hand in mine, and we made our way to what would be our new canteen for the next few days.

The soldiers hadn't finished setting it up yet, but Daisy was helping the soldiers coordinate some meals, and she handed us some food, several large sandwiches made up, and a potato salad. Carb heavy, but just the thing we needed after we'd been using our powers so much. There was also more appropriate food for Nuri, Sen, and Roth laid out.

Once again, I thanked Daisy, always impressed by how she could go from deadly sharpshooter to chef and organizer in the space of a few seconds.

We were still in the middle of eating when I heard the sound of a large vehicle pulling up outside and someone shouting. I grabbed another sandwich and walked out of the tent with it and toward the sound of commotion.

As the major had predicted, a large muscular man got out of a huge pickup, demanding to know why soldiers were on his land.

"It's all right," I called to the nearest soldier to him and the one who was the target of the rage. "Everyone is here because of me and my mythicals."

On cue, Zephyr shifted from his human form into dragon form. The guy stepped back, his eyes going wide. The soldier smirked for a fraction of a second before going back to his post.

"I'm Aella," I said. "And this is one of my bonded mythicals, Zephyr the dragon. Do I understand correctly that you're the landowner?"

The man nodded, still staring at Zephyr.

"Do you want to have some dinner with me, such as it is, and we'll discuss what's happening here?" I asked, holding up the sandwich I was still clutching. "Using my abilities makes me extra hungry, and I had to fly quite a way to get here."

He looked between me, the food, and the dragon, and then back to me again.

"What did you say your name was?" he asked as I turned to walk toward the tent, and he came up beside me.

Zephyr backed up to let us pass, giving the guy some space now he seemed friendly. I offered the man my name for a second time, and I also introduced Zephyr again and my three other mythicals as we entered the tent.

Daisy didn't hesitate to bring some more food over, offering the man a selection from everything prepared as I used my abilities to pull his seat out for him and mine at the same time.

"You're that elf who's been on TV, ain't ya?" he asked a moment later.

"Yes, probably. I'm quite special for an elf, and I have the last dragon left on Earth as far as we're aware of."

"Well, I'm Jack. Jack Mitchell. I must say I've watched what you've been doing with some interest. Well, the wife more so. She said you could fly without the dragon. I wasn't sure I believed it, but you telling me it's true?"

"Yes, Mr. Mitchell," I replied as I rose into the air.

His eyes went wide again, and he sat down.

"The wife is gonna be so excited when I tell her I've seen you fly," he said as he shook his head.

Then he reached for his plate and took a bite of a sandwich. I let him enjoy it and sat back down so I could eat as well.

"So, tell me. What's going on here? I don't want to sound rude, but you are on my land, and I didn't give you permission."

"I'm sorry about that. We needed to move fast, and we didn't have time to warn you."

"Warn me?" He stopped eating, his sandwich halfway to his mouth.

"It's okay. You're not in any danger. Not right now, and it was a preemptive thing. We're hoping no one will ever be in danger."

"There some funky artifact under the ground there where you've been digging?"

I sat back, trying to figure out what I should tell this guy. Although the major had made it clear I wasn't supposed to let him know much, I needed to give him something to go on or he would keep asking more questions.

"It's not exactly an artifact," I said eventually, taking the plunge.

I told him about the portals, how there was something

evil on the other side but they didn't know about this one, and that we planned to rescue some elves through it and then close it again.

As I talked, his eyes got wider, and he became more uncomfortable.

"I'm not sure I like the sound of there being a portal to another world on my land. Especially if some twisted creature is trying to wage a war on our planet through it."

"I don't much like it either, which is why we hope to close or bury it again once we're done."

"And I'm guessing you don't want me to tell anyone about this?"

"Nope. There are elves on our planet. Only a few, to be clear, but they would want to see this opened if they heard about it. I have to ask you not to tell your wife."

"Then why did you tell me?" he asked.

"So you'd know the whole reason when I tell you that I'd like to buy this land from you, or at least this section of it. There's a building down there, and one of the best ways I can protect the portal long-term is to restore the building and station elves here. I don't want to do that without offering you a decent price for it. You can tell everyone I'm restoring an old elven settlement, and I can protect this entire planet."

He sat back, exhaling as he thought about it.

"And you'll pay me a fair price?"

"I will. I don't want you to be stubborn and insist on a massive amount, but I won't deny that I like the idea of restoring the building. The site is worth more to me than you. I'm sure we can find a price that works for both of us as long as we stay reasonable."

"And it will help hide what's here and keep folks safe?"

"That's what I do—protect those who need it."

"All right. The wife likes you, and she said that was the kind of person you are. Someone who tries to look out for the little guy. Will I have these soldiers here all the time, though?"

"They will be here for now, but I hope I won't always need their aid. This place would then have people living here," I said as I got up. Although I wanted to talk more to him, I'd done enough. I autographed a scrap of paper for his wife, then I said goodbye to the man, and one of the soldiers escorted him out.

I wasn't sure I'd done the right thing, but I felt good about it. I noticed Cherisse had entered the tent and was sitting and eating.

"Nicely handled," she said. "And thank you."

I had no idea how to respond. It felt as if something had shifted between us. Cherisse had seen me put my money on the line, despite the possibility that I'd have a clash with the general and the President, to offer her and Amcika a new home similar to the one they'd lost.

I knew they needed it. The Amcika elves and mythicals were our allies. They mattered too.

CHAPTER FIVE

As I stood before the pillars once more, I tried not to worry about how this would turn out. The general hadn't been happy that I'd told the landowner what was going on here. He hadn't been happy that I'd decided to buy the land. It had taken the President stepping in and me explaining it to him to resolve it.

The President hadn't been happy either, although he had understood why I wanted to buy it and not have it controlled by the military. Especially after I had conceded that while the portal was a threat to humanity, I would still allow his soldiers to work with us to keep it safe. Making it clear I wasn't shutting him out so much as making sure Cherisse and her elves had a place they could call home again had sealed the deal.

The next difficult discussion was what to do with the portal. The pillars stood over it, and we couldn't open it, but I wanted to go through. I didn't want to wait.

"They're ready," a soldier said, disturbing me.

I nodded and headed to the small command tent,

knowing that I was about to meet with many important people.

Ronan, Minsheng, Cherisse, and the major were there waiting for me. Zephyr had taken human form, and we gathered around a screen showing us the general and the President.

"Thank you for all that you're doing," the President said as soon as he saw me. "Tell me what you want to do."

Everyone looked at me, giving me the space to explain everything I knew and what I was hoping to achieve. It wasn't a great plan. It had its risks, and I acknowledged them while also suggesting many mitigations.

"It feels as if we have little choice but to proceed despite the risks. If we can strengthen our defenses and weaken the dark elf's, it's a good trade, but it concerns me that we could be giving him yet another way to attack us."

"It concerns me too. The Sanctuary is doing everything they can to figure out how to close the portals and rebuild the pillars again should we need to."

The President nodded. My assurance was unnecessary. The Sanctuary had been doing that since Amcika had opened the first portal. While there were hints here and there in books about closing a portal, nothing suggested how to keep it permanently closed or how to rebuild the pillars that protected it.

We might never know how to do that, but I was determined to continue. There was always the option to bury the portal like the Mexican one.

It wasn't ideal but, it was worth the risk in my mind. I bit my lip and clenched my fists to keep from fidgeting with my hands while I waited for the go-ahead to continue.

Ronan, Minsheng, Simon, and Cherisse agreed with me. I knew that at least two of them would try to persuade me to act anyway if the President didn't give his approval. I didn't want to be in that position.

If I was going through the portal to rescue some mythicals, then I wanted as much support as I could get, especially from a military force that had conducted these sorts of missions before.

"Okay. Do what you need to. I'll send you some soldiers with experience in this matter, and more equipment. Major, General, I expect you to keep updating me and make a list of what you and the soldiers I send think is necessary for this mission, as well as the continued support of Aella, Amcika, and the Sanctuary in this matter. I want to see this succeed if we're going to take this risk. Make it worth it. For all our sakes."

"Yes, Sir," I said before anyone else could.

The President looked at me with a slight smirk on his face before he gave us a salute.

I didn't relax until he was gone.

"Sounds like it's time to break those pillars," the general said when he was left to pick up the next section. "Go do what you must. Let the major know of any practical needs you have, and we'll do our best to source it for you."

This was all I needed to hear, and I hurried away from the meeting again, not sure I wanted to do anything other than mentally prepare for the task ahead. The last time we'd broken pillars, Zephyr had ended up doing it. This time we were going to attempt it together, and hopefully from outside the forcefield.

Minsheng was soon to come after us, his device in hand and a frown on his face.

"Something wrong?" I asked.

"Not exactly. I'm concerned for your welfare. You and Zephyr. The elves designed these pillars to be incredibly hard to break so that they could only be breached by those strong enough to face the threat on the other side."

"If that's true, then they didn't make them strong enough." I thought of how Zephyr and I could reach them from outside most of the forcefields. Our range with the elements was far greater than any other elves, however.

It was something that the makers couldn't have been able to predict. They knew a Henera was coming but not how powerful they'd be exactly or in what ways they would be more powerful.

I also knew that the darkness on the other side was stronger than I was. It made sense that he would be. He'd had millennia to practice, and he'd been fighting elves for a significant part of the time. It was no surprise.

Minsheng studied me while I thought and prepared for what we were about to do. Despite my attitude, it really wasn't going to be easy.

I considered putting on the helmet or getting some of the tablets and crystals we'd been charging up over the last few days, but I couldn't waste the power if this were something I could do myself. We might need the backup power later, especially if we had to fight anything to get to the elves who needed us.

"Are you sure you want to do this?" Minsheng asked me. "It's dangerous to open another portal. If he—"

"I know. And I know you're worried about us and

everyone else here. I have this power. I'm supposed to be the Henera. This important elven savior. If all I do is show off, scare people when they disagree with me, and hide instead of helping, then I'm wasting what I have and not worthy of it."

Minsheng exhaled as he looked me in the eyes. "I feared that you'd say something like that, but I'm proud of you. Even if I'm afraid you might get yourself killed, you're right."

"Thank you," I replied. "You've always trusted me and encouraged me and the others. You've believed in us from the beginning."

"And I always will. No matter what. You've become more than I hoped you would. Now, I'll get out of your way and let you do what you do best."

Zephyr came up beside me, and I took his hand. We were going to do this together. As soon as Minsheng stepped back, his devices monitoring our progress and the portal to make sure that no one on the other side noticed what we were doing, we got ready.

We opted to reach for the fire pillar first, needing to get the closest to that one because it was our weakest element. I concentrated on feeling through the pillar for the center. My concentration and power combined with Zephyr's the way the dark elves had been showing us so we could combine our power effectively.

It took time to push through the forcefield with our minds. We connected to the pillar and the center. There appeared to be a crystal in the middle of each pillar. The carved symbols and runes on the outside hummed with a power of their own.

It made for a significant challenge. The pillar was like fighting an extremely competent elf. An elf who was trying to tear us apart if we got too close. However, our minds were getting used to this type of mental battle, and we soon pushed past the defenses. By the time we'd begun attacking the crystal in the center, the strain was starting to show.

My mind felt the pressure, but we broke through the final layer of defense, and the pillar shattered, giving way before us. Panting, I let go of everything, grateful that this time we could act outside the forcefield and not have to defend ourselves at the same time.

"Interesting," Minsheng said, staring at the device in his hands. "There was an energy burst as you broke that. As if they're energy powered and the crystal in the center stores elemental energy."

"So they're probably powered. Does that mean they can run out?"

Minsheng looked at me as it dawned on us what that might mean. How much power did the pillars need to maintain the forcefield, and could they be drained? Would the elves who put them into place have thought of this, and how were we going to stand a chance to replicate it?

"Do you think you could break some of these without shattering them into so many tiny pieces?"

I almost winced, not sure I could do that. I didn't control the attack. It was something I had to explode.

We could try the air pillar next, Zephyr said. *It's the one you have the most control over.*

He had a good point. If we were going to be gentle with

a pillar, it made sense to use my best element, although I had planned to save that until the end.

Instead, I focused on the pillar with the air runes on it. Zephyr joined his control with mine, but it was the briefest of connections. I wanted to be as careful as I could, so this time I moved more slowly, feeling my way across the forcefield and into the pillar. I found the edge of the crystal, not fighting it for control yet.

It was a delicate construction, and I could see why it blew up when I had been more forceful. I pulled back and decided the best way was to pull it apart and disarm it yet keep it stable.

The runes were an intricate network that channeled the power through to the crystal. I could focus on them more now that I was aware of them. Zephyr continued to move with me, letting me guide our combined strength. Once again, I delved into the pillar.

The resistance was beginning to get familiar enough, and the element so much more easily controlled that I soon worked my way deeper. This time, instead of pushing to take control of the crystal in the middle and stop it from exerting power, I gently felt the power inside. As it exerted energy to control the forcefield, I attempted to redirect it.

Zephyr was working with me, trying to help me pull out the first strand of energy and channel it. At first, it seemed as if it was working, and I started controlling more air and spinning it around the chamber. We kept it gentle, simply moving the air, but I could feel it picking up speed.

We need to be careful, Zephyr said. *We can't let it get out of control.*

I'm being careful, I replied, but I could feel what he was worried about. The energy was coming out faster than before and increasing as if it was too full, and I'd given it a way out. It was pushing out faster.

We channeled it, moving outside with my control to use a bigger area of air. The power continued to grow until I felt as if I was going to burst, my bonds growing stronger and my body filling with the energy. More filled me until I thought I was going to burst.

This isn't working. There's too much power.

Zephyr pulled back to unhook from the crystal, but it gripped on, keeping us there, flowing into us.

The pain built up inside as there was simply too much power. Following Zephyr's lead, I pulled away to disconnect. It didn't work for me, either. As I tried again, the pain grew. It was like trying to fight the dark elf's grip, but it was much stronger.

We need to blow it up like the others. This isn't working.

I resisted. This wasn't going well, but I was close to succeeding. I reached for more air and used up as much of the energy as I could, pumping it outside as I did. I heard the sound of running footsteps, but it was hard to turn, and I couldn't see who it was.

"There's a hurricane starting out there. Is that you?" the major asked.

I frowned, the pain and concentration too much to reply. Zephyr was right. This had to stop. Too many people were in danger.

Gritting my teeth, I fought against the pain and worked with Zephyr to fight the control. I wanted to stop it, but it was holding on too tightly. The pain intensified, each part of me feeling as if it was going to tear apart.

I whimpered, struggling to hold on until Nuri landed on my shoulder. The firebird sent calm my way and began walking me through the same process I'd used for the dark elf and how I broke his contact. Fighting directly against it never worked.

The contact had to be severed in a more roundabout way, using less power, more precision, and a lot more subtlety. Slowly I disconnected, lessening the energy coming out of the pillar and into the air around me. The pain continued to grow, far too much energy still trying to store itself in my body, but I managed to lessen the flow with the help of my mythicals.

I was about to disconnect from the pillar entirely, my mind and body in so much pain I wanted it to be over when the crystal and pillar exploded. Stone fragments went flying, whipped around by the spinning vortex until I felt a new pain.

My mind and reactions took over, slowing the debris and trying to keep it away from my mythicals, Minsheng, and me. At first, I thought I would fail, and it would cut us to pieces, but it was as if I was supercharged, and the air obeyed me so swiftly that it was soon perfectly still inside the cavern.

Exhaling, I looked at Minsheng. He was sporting several new cuts and bruises from the combination of debris, and I must look similar, my skin stinging and my body shaking.

"I think the pillars work in a very different way to normal crystals," I said, not sure what else to say.

It was an understatement and probably not a helpful

sentence, but Minsheng nodded as if this was entirely reasonable.

Without thinking, I took control of Minsheng's body near the largest cut. Seconds later, I'd cleaned it, encouraged the body to heal faster, and started working on the next one.

He stared as I worked in silence, using the spare energy inside me to help him.

"Thank you," he said when I finished and pulled back.

It wasn't a perfect job, but I'd done what I could. The awe in Minsheng's words made me feel as if I'd managed to pay for what had happened. After all, it had been my fault. If I could help people, I needed to.

CHAPTER SIX

It was emotional to find myself standing in front of so many I knew. Some had been at my side for a long time. Others were relatively new faces, but they were all looking to me for leadership and a plan. I had to lead them to an unknown land to rescue some other elves and possibly other mythicals. I had no idea what to expect.

I'd broken all four pillars. I'd tried to keep them intact, but the energy within them had proved too much for me to do much more than explode each one with a bit more control. There was no way I wanted to repeat the incident I'd almost caused with the air pillar. It had nearly led to me destroying our camp outside this underground building, and Minsheng, my mythicals, and I were sporting several cuts and bruises because of it.

We hadn't yet opened the portal, however. It was supposed to be far easier than the pillars, but it still required magic, and now that it came to it, I wasn't sure I wanted to continue.

The last portal opened had been behind closed doors in

the mountain. It opened after Zephyr broke the pillars to save my life. I had no idea how to do it or if there was something else I needed to know. All I had to go on were Zephyr's memories of closing portals and a few passages in different books. A few elves still alive had relatives who had seen it, but no one had lived through it but Nuri.

I took a deep breath and looked around the cavern. Not everyone approved of me opening this one up. The President was reluctant but knew he couldn't stop me. Thankfully, he hadn't tried.

The Sanctuary and the organization were strangely supportive. They saw bringing more elves to our side of the portals, out from the control of the dark elf holding power on the other world, as being our duty and to our benefit.

Worried, anxious, and nervous faces looked back at me as I scanned the team I had. They were trying to hide it, for the most part, especially the team of soldiers who had to train for this in a very different way, but I could tell that they weren't quite as calm. It was almost as if the air around everyone picked up on their tension and transmitted it to me.

"Thank you, everyone, for agreeing to help me with this," I said. "I want to say again that any of you who wish to remain here may. We will command no one to go through this portal. You're here for a reason. You're the best at what you do and the allies I would wish for in many situations. There are a bunch of mythicals who need our help."

Everyone's eyes locked on me as I spoke, making me feel self-conscious. No matter how often I led a team into battle, it never got any easier. I tried not to think too hard about it, however. They needed me to encourage them and seem confident.

"As soon as this portal is open, we're going to head out. Scouts with me and then everyone else fifteen minutes after. We don't want to take long, and we want to move fast on the other side. We should have a guide of some sort, but not until we get into enemy territory."

With that, I moved to stand beside Cherisse. She'd opened a portal before and had since run me through the process. Together we were going to open this one. Zephyr, in human form, also stood beside me, and then Seth joined us on the other side. We would each focus on an element, drawing the power from a gemstone or tablet.

Then the four of us, our bonded mythicals, and a small group of soldiers and elves were going to go straight through. It was risky, but it was also the best way to give the dark elf and everyone working for him the least opportunity to detect the activity and the open portal. We knew they weren't guarding it. It would have to be enough.

Concentrating, I focused on the target in hand. I connected to the air near the portal device and reached deeper for the strange combination of elements sitting at the heart of it.

Feeling the other three elementals working with me was an interesting moment. Two of them had either once shown a great animosity toward me or tried to kill me more than once. Here they were, alongside the love of my life, trying to open a portal. If anyone had told me I'd be here with this group earlier in the year, I'd have thought they were joking.

But it seemed my life was fated to go in strange directions. I was possibly only along for the ride.

It didn't take long for Zephyr to also be ready beside me, but we had to wait for Seth and Cherisse, the pair of them struggling to control their respective element in the device. Although it would have been easier for me to do the whole thing, Cherisse knew what she was doing, and I didn't want to drain myself or a gemstone. That meant doing it together with patience and extra time.

As soon as everyone else was ready, I pushed forward, taking the lead as we pulled out the threads from the center of this crystal, stretching them toward the outside of the portal. It was like constructing the main strands of a spider web, each one coming out from the center, but we didn't stop with a few. We kept going, filling in the gaps, working as a group until the center glowed.

The portal remembered its connections as well, the task growing easier as we progressed until it felt as if it was doing it for us. I could feel the energy it was draining, seeming to suck it out of me on its own as the circle filled more. It grew brighter until I was struggling to look at it, and it felt as if it was rushing to complete itself.

"Hold it steady," Cherisse said a moment later as Seth got ahead of himself, and a spark of fire flared in one section of the almost complete circle.

He exhaled and nodded almost imperceptibly. Trying not to worry about it and giving the fire elemental time to recover, I held steady a moment as well, but he soon got back on track. Within another minute, the portal took over, reconnecting with no input from us whatsoever. The connection didn't end, however.

I thought it was sucking more energy from us, but I soon realized it was doing the opposite now. It was as if the bonds formed from this world to the elven homeworld were giving off energy. Once more, I felt energy entering my body, the sensation making Seth's eyes widen, the only one of us who had no experience with it.

After less than ten minutes from start to end, we were done. The portal device let go of the connections for us as if there was nothing to connect to in the same way anymore. I watched it as it began spinning, but it became a blur.

Another couple of seconds and the portal connected. I could feel the edge of it and the connection and energy it represented. I was surprised it didn't feel the same as the portal in the mountain Amcika had called home.

The moment it was complete, a few people applauded, and the first group that was going through the portal with us stepped forward. Sen bounded onto my shoulder and Nuri landed on Zephyr's, leaving Roth to trot between us. Cherisse, Minsheng, Seth, Ronan, the major, and three soldiers also came forward, sporting tranquilizer guns and whatever other weaponry they favored.

I stepped ahead of them and walked into the portal before I could reveal how nervous I felt or get more anxious while thinking about everything that might go wrong.

The sensation of being in the portal was strange. It was like stepping into a waterfall or trying to lie down in a fast-flowing river. Something was constantly rushing past, but the path of progression was in an entirely different direction. My mind could still reach out to the elements, but I couldn't control anything.

Although I'd felt how long it took for my mind to travel through the portal and knew it wasn't quick, I was pretty sure it took longer for my mind and body to go through together. Finally, the rushing slowed, and I found my body stepping out of the portal into a barren wasteland. I blinked in the blinding sun a few times.

I was so overwhelmed by the different smells, the bright light, and the absence of noise now that I was through the portal that I couldn't do much but stand there.

Instinctively, my mind reached out for the air around me and began trying to shape it and form the usual protective barrier around my body. It felt weird connecting to the foreign elements. Elves had marked them in a whole new way.

It took me several minutes to figure out how to connect to the four elements around me before I realized we were standing out in the open without the ability to defend ourselves. Once I had a barrier around the entire group, I looked around.

In every direction I looked, it was as if we were in a desert-like wasteland, here and there a gnarled bush of some kind, but nothing else moving or living.

There are no birds, Zephyr said. *No insects. Nothing but a few odd bushes and wind.*

It didn't take me long to realize he was right. It was strange. It made the silence around us seem deafening, and I took several steps forward as Minsheng pulled out familiar tools and devices.

"Find somewhere nearby to keep watch on the portal

and wait for the next group," the major told two of the soldiers with him before they checked if their radios would work in this new environment.

When the comm crackled to life, proving that messages would get through, I exhaled. We'd have that when we split up the group. I had another one clipped to my belt and pulled it off to test it as well.

After more checks and quiet conversations, we agreed that several of us should head in the direction we thought we needed to go. At the same time, I let go of everything but the barrier I intended to move with most of us and reached out as far as I could in a circle.

Although elves had marked the elements in a way I didn't recognize, they were free of current control. No one was close to us, and I'd know if anyone did arrive or come nearby, hopefully before anyone saw us.

Despite that, none of us dared make much noise, and we stayed close together. Zephyr slipped his hand into mine. He was still in human form, not wanting to draw attention to being a dragon or make a larger, easier target to spot if others were nearby. It also allowed us to use his abilities in a small group, which would be important.

I didn't have detailed instructions, but we made our way across the rocky sand. The landscape slowly changed, the bushes growing more frequent, some with more leaves and less stunted. However, there were still no animals, and it was a while before we saw or I felt anything ahead.

I stopped suddenly, feeling another mind brush against my control. Quickly pulling back mentally, I signaled that I'd felt something, and we crouched and moved slowly toward the nearest bushes.

Taking a deep breath to calm down, I reached forward again, but I brushed against the control and wasn't sure I dared push any farther.

Sen go see, my myconid said as she bounded off my shoulder.

Before I could do anything to stop her, she ran off, bouncing quickly between bushes and peering at what lay ahead of her. I wanted to call her back, but Zephyr put a hand on my shoulder and sent comforting thoughts my way. I exhaled and tried to ignore my fears and worries.

Instead, I closed my eyes and followed what Sen could see. Our bond was able to project what her small body could pick up on. She could move so fast and repeatedly rushed between bushes and then stopped again that I was pretty sure I'd get motion sickness if I watched through her eyes too much, but it didn't take long for her to find what had disturbed me.

There was a small patrol unit of four dark elves, and they were coming toward us on a dirt track. Sen tucked herself behind a bush nearby and held as still as she could. The four elves each had an elemental symbol tattooed on their arms and were marching along in time like robots.

It was chilling and relentless, and I was pretty sure that if Sen had moved a muscle or been moving before they'd got close that they would have discovered her. They must have been using their abilities to feel around them, but she had hidden her little plant body well enough from their senses that they hurried right past her.

Grateful for the tiny dryad and the way she could aid us, we waited until the patrol had disappeared into the distance before any of us dared to move again, including

Sen. While finding the patrol added to the danger, it was also proof that we were going in the right direction. Finding a road had been my first goal. Now we would head after the patrol.

Although I was eager to keep on, I held everyone back. While Sen and I could detect patrols and avoid them, the group following me didn't have that advantage. Most of them were soldiers and elves, and there weren't any other plant-based mythicals who could scout ahead without being detected.

Apparently, animals would stand out here as much as we did.

CHAPTER SEVEN

By the time the larger team joined us, there had been three more patrols. There was no way we could get a group as large as we were past that many dark elves without serious planning and some way of shielding and hiding or luring the patrols away from the road.

After a swift discussion with Zephyr, we ordered everyone else back to the portal and stayed where we were to make sure no one detected the group.

"I must say, I don't think I've ever seen you be so cautious," Cherisse said when we were almost back at the portal, most of our soldiers and elves having gone through it.

"I can't let *him* find out about this portal. As much as I want to rescue these elves, we'll put everyone on Earth in danger if we let him know."

"So, you're thinking about the people on Earth?"

"What do you mean?" I replied, hearing the hint of anger in her voice.

"You tried again and again to stop me from opening a

portal because you thought it wasn't up to us to decide that for everyone on Earth. However, as soon as you had a reason to open a portal, you went ahead and did it."

"I know, and I understand why that would make you angry," I replied. "It's very similar. I still don't know if we've done the right thing by opening this one, but one of them was already open. We have not figured out how to control or close either yet, and the dark elf doesn't know about this one."

"It's still deciding that Earth will take the risk."

"It is. I can only offer an apology if that seems hypocritical." I stopped far enough away from everyone but Zephyr that we could continue talking without them hearing if Cherisse wanted.

She studied me. She had a point, and my apology was sincere, but the stakes had also changed since I'd made my earlier statement. As had everything I knew about the enemy. Nuri had changed how well I could defend against him.

Cherisse had also learned more since she'd tried to open the first portal. The truth was that neither of us had been entirely right. We'd clashed and fought, and we had to be allies. There was a dark elf who knew there was a portal open, and I had a feeling he wasn't going to rest until he found a way through or we stopped him.

"You know you're going to have to face him someday, don't you? That it's too late to stop that fight now," she said eventually, showing she'd followed my train of thought.

I nodded, not having accepted it until that moment. It wasn't a risk for humanity to open another portal when war was inevitable. It was an attempt to give ourselves better odds, with the chance that we might make our final odds worse instead.

"Okay, let's figure out how to get past those patrols and come back and rescue some elves. If nothing else, we're all on board with that."

I motioned for Cherisse to head toward the portal first, knowing I held the barrier that would keep us safe until the last moment. It was disappointing to be going back to Earth so soon, but we had to. We had learned something about this planet, and we had to make sure we didn't take risks we didn't need to.

Cherisse was right about one thing. We should be careful.

There were several happy faces when we got back. We encouraged everyone who wasn't essential to get some rest or food and made our way to the tent that served as our command center. Within seconds, the general was on the computer. We talked about what had happened and what we'd seen.

By the time I'd explained everything and answered his questions, the mood in the room was serious. The truth was clear. It was going to be difficult to rescue anyone on the other side of the portal. It was also clear that we ought to try.

If it was as barren as it looked, they were struggling. Although Earth wasn't perfect, it could sustain them while we figured out how to defeat the dark elf.

"If we're going to make this work and make sure that the people who agree to fund this sort of thing want to, we need to think of additional selling points," the general said, sounding more enthusiastic than I expected.

"What did you have in mind, sir?" the major replied as he sat forward.

"Soil samples, plant samples. Anything that might be of benefit to humanity, especially any tech."

I nodded without hesitation as Minsheng made notes.

"I'll see what other gear I can get you that might aid you in hiding and preventing detection, although I have a feeling that something mythical based is likely to be of more use," the general finished before deciding to leave us to it.

Once again, I was struck by how little anyone was objecting to what we were doing. Given the level of danger, I expected more caution. Of course, the portal was open now. It was only a matter of time before the dark elf found it and tried to make it his.

Minsheng, Chris, and Simon dismissed me and put their heads together to develop tech that would get us past a patrol, even if it was only a small group.

Not sure what to do and not particularly tired or feeling as if I needed sleep, I made sure Roth, Sen, and Nuri were safe to rest and made my way back into the underground building to find the portal cave.

I stared at it for a while, annoyed that I couldn't communicate to the female elf I had been talking to through the Texas portal. As far as we could tell, the portals were a long way away from each other on the planets. If they were in the same direction was an entirely different matter.

Zephyr slipped his arm around me.

You're worried, he said, his voice sounding gentle.

It's a lot to ask of people for someone we don't really know. If we're caught over there and trapped... I trailed off, struggling to think of something I could say out loud and still not be so terrifying. I didn't want to focus on the negative, but others had trapped me somewhere one too many times.

This was always going to be dangerous. We know that. You've done a good job of leading us on so far, and you'll do a good job this time.

Zephyr's words were reassuring, but I thought of Lorcan and how he'd died, and then Ascan a short time later. It was a while ago, and so much had happened since. The pain of losing someone I'd called a friend had dulled, but I suspected it would never entirely fade.

People may die, but we'll do what we can to prevent it. We can't take that fear into another battle. We have to go in confidently and learn from our mistakes. We can accept what each death teaches us and try to prevent more.

That's not the most comforting of speeches, I replied, but the corner of my mouth twitched up. He'd said something similar before, and he had a point.

It is what it is, and we can only be who we are. It's always been enough in the past, and it will be enough in the future.

Zephyr pulled me in closer to rest my head on his shoulder.

A moment later, there was a cough from behind.

"I hope I'm not interrupting," Chris said as we turned to him. "But I think we've managed to modify some camo gear the soldiers had and added an element that will act a bit like the Sanctuary shields. You won't look or feel like you're there as long as none of you are moving."

I lifted my eyebrows as he held up some large swathes of fabric that looked a bit like capes with hoods.

"They've not been tested, but it's that or nothing," he added as he held them out for Zephyr and me to take.

They had tailored the capes to about the right height. They were an inch or so above the floor and billowed around us.

"It wasn't easy to get everyone something quickly, so Daisy and I made a large cape design. We figured if you saw trouble, you could stop and crouch and hope to blend in. Minsheng said the dwarves in the organization might be able to send over some enchanted brooches or something that will make the camo even more effective."

"Like the cloaks the hobbits had," Zephyr replied.

Grinning from ear to ear, Chris nodded.

Although it felt strange to be accepting more help from the gnome, I found myself feeling grateful. If the organization could make the cloaks protect us and hide us in multiple ways, our whole mission would be safer.

Hope filled my heart again. Maybe we could do this after all. Maybe we could rescue these elven refugees and put ourselves in a stronger position the next time the dark elf came knocking on our portal.

There were still quite a few preparations to make, and I also needed to rest if we were going to venture out swiftly. First thing the following morning, a smaller team was standing in the portal room, each of us draped in a camouflage cape that sported a small dragon broach around the neck. It looked strange to see everyone wearing identical clothing on the outside.

I was used to it with the soldiers, but seeing the elves wearing it and a cloak styled for the Ronan's centaur body was entirely different. For the first time, we looked like a team. I noticed the dragon broach on Zephyr's cloak that glowed in the dim light.

"Don't worry," Minsheng said as I covered it with my hand. "It won't glow for anyone you're hiding from. It makes it easier for us to spot you. It's a command feature the dwarves bake into their tech."

Minsheng's explanation gave me more questions than it answered, but it wasn't the time to ask them. If the glow wasn't going to be visible to others, then it wasn't.

I surveyed our team. Cherisse, Seth, Minsheng, Ronan, and the major stood in front of a squad of four soldiers. Roth was beside Zephyr, with Nuri and Sen resting on them. Roth and Sen had a cloak, and Nuri had a strange hood and some lightweight fabric that hooked over his wings. We'd agreed that in most situations, he would hide under one of our cloaks.

Sen beamed from inside hers, intermittently practicing hiding in it and almost disappearing from view. I had to concentrate to see her, although she was wearing desert colors in a rock building of an entirely different shade.

Erlan, Emily, and Daisy were staying behind with the rest of the soldiers, plus Simon and Sierrathen. They would protect the portal from anyone who might get behind us and discover it. Hopefully, no one would, but we prepared for that anyway.

With each of us carrying a bag full of food, camping supplies in case we were out there overnight, medical essentials for any refugees we came across, spare ammo for the weapons, and water containers, we were ready to go. We didn't have much water because we wouldn't struggle to get more from the world around us. Cherisse, Zephyr, and I could control it.

Once again, I'd gone over the directions the elf on the other side of the Texas portal had given me and committed it to memory. It wasn't complicated, and people were supposed to be expecting and looking out for us, but I had no idea if we needed to walk for a few hours or a few days to get to these refugees.

All we could do was attempt to find them and hope it worked out and avoid patrols, soldiers, and anyone else we couldn't be sure of along the way.

I stepped through the portal first again, with Zephyr not far behind me. The travel length and arriving on the other end was easier to handle this time, my mind coping better with the strange sensation of being everywhere and nowhere at once.

On this trip, I was also wearing sunglasses, giving my eyes less pressure to adjust and allowing me to focus on forming a barrier around the portal first. Once I'd connected mentally and had the protection for everyone else in place, I checked to see if anyone was nearby and if someone or something might see us.

Once more, I was struck by how silent everything was. The only sound for the next minute or so was the portal spitting out Zephyr where I'd expected. There was simply no animal life, and it made me wonder if Roth, Sen, and Nuri were possibly in more danger here than the rest of us. Even if they weren't, I was sure that we wanted to be careful in case it drew unwanted attention.

It didn't take long for the rest of the party to arrive, emerging safe in the knowledge that my barrier would be up and protecting them. As before, I reached out with my mind and felt through the air, making sure no one moved in it anywhere near us.

I was grateful for the rest. I found it easier to connect this time, and it gave me time to appreciate the strange marked element. Air had been the least marked element in the mountain. Probably thanks to the mountain needing to have a constant throughput of air to keep everyone inside alive.

Here, however, it was as if someone had once held it and kept hold of it for the power it represented. It made me grateful that the Sanctuary had a small number of elves, and they weren't in the same place for long all at once. This hadn't happened on Earth. I hoped it never did.

CHAPTER EIGHT

The second advantage of having only a small team on the planet was needing a smaller barrier to protect us. I didn't have to work as hard to keep the edge of it cold or stop it from moving in the breeze that blew across the desolate area. I was grateful for my abilities as we made our way across the desert to the dirt track.

Sen was bounding in front, keeping an eye out for patrols while I walked farther back. I was still reaching ahead with my mind, and I could feel Zephyr's mind behind us, making sure no one snuck up on us while we were focused elsewhere.

With everyone trudging along, not saying anything since we didn't know what dangers lay ahead, the mood was somber. We were used to difficult situations, but this was a new level of unknown. It wasn't easy to handle.

There were so many ways this mission could go wrong compared to previous ones. Getting stuck on a foreign planet was a possibility that made me shudder the moment I thought of it. A part of me could understand why

Cherisse had wanted to open the portal and make contact. If people had been separated from loved ones and still had connections to each other, then reuniting them was a worthy goal.

Getting them off a planet controlled by an evil elf was another matter, however.

We had to balance it with not wrecking Earth the way they had destroyed this planet. Or ravaged. Possibly both.

Our planet was under strain. It was important that I didn't add to that burden. It meant I had yet another factor to consider when rescuing elves on this mission.

The simplest solution is to defeat the dark elf here, Zephyr said as I scanned the road with my mind. We were still clear of approaching guards.

Although I was leading, my people had fanned out, none of us wanting to get in the others' way. I was keeping us safe, and it made little difference with a group this small if we were in a tight unit or spread out a bit. The energy required to maintain something this basic was not a problem.

Of course, fights and challenges to my control would drain me more quickly if we weren't careful and had to stop guards from reporting our presence to the dark elf, but we hoped to avoid confrontations.

We neared the road. Sen was near the edge, keeping a lookout. Given the frequency of patrols we'd encountered the first time we were on the planet, it wouldn't be long before we would put our new cloaks to the test.

With each passing minute, I grew tenser and more worried that they wouldn't function and we wouldn't know until it was too late.

Have faith in the mythicals we work with, Zephyr said. *The organization and everyone else who works with them, the Sanctuary, and Amcika, are full of mythicals who have trained and learned all they could to help in these sorts of situations.*

I know. I am aware we've trained for moments like this too. But we can't afford for this to go wrong. Enough has gone south lately. We need something to work.

You might not have enough faith in yourself, but I assure you I do.

I exhaled and nodded, sending waves of gratitude to Zephyr through the bond. I was unable to put what I felt into words. I was concentrating again, knowing I was partially responsible for keeping everyone safe, when the control of another air elf brushed against mine.

I frowned and pulled back, letting Sen know and holding up my hand for everyone to stop. Within a second, we were stationary. Everyone crouched as they pulled their hoods up. I waited for Sen to let me know what she could see ahead.

It didn't take long for her to spot a patrol coming up the road. I held up my hands again, sticking up four fingers and motioning in the direction the patrol was heading. It wasn't perfect communication, but it was the best I could think to do.

Slowly, we moved to the nearest bush. Nuri landed on the ground in front of me as I swept the cloak I wore over him. Not sure what else to do, I verified that I was covered by my cloak and checked that everyone else was as well. Even Sen had draped herself in the garment, and I struggled to focus my gaze on everyone.

Even knowing where everyone had been crouching a

moment before, my brain refused to see them now. They were just strange shadows, not there if I looked directly at them but visible out of the corner of my eye.

I could still feel my bond with my mythicals and see Nuri, but that was as confident as I got that I was seeing something contradictory to what I knew.

With any luck, it would be good enough to fool the patrol elves as well. I noticed them slow as they came closer, one of the lead dark elves in the patrol looking over to where we were. His eyes followed the line of bushes in front of me but did not notice my form crouched right by it.

The whole group of dark elves then picked up on the strange behavior and also slowed. None of them spoke, but the lead elf didn't move on again yet and eventually stopped not far from us.

I barely dared to breathe, let alone move, and hoped that no one else did anything that might give us away. It was clear that the dark elves were struggling to see us as well, aware that something had changed but unable to pinpoint our positions.

I was used to the feel of others taking control while training in the warehouse, Sanctuary, or at the Texas portal. The dark elf reached out toward my mind and the area in general, however. It forced me to stop holding a barrier and give way before him to keep our presence undetected. I felt vulnerable and exposed, as if he could look through my clothes and see where I was.

I didn't do anything but wait, and the dark elves eventually grew less interested and appeared as if they'd march again.

My heart hammered in my chest at the best of times, but while under the scrutiny of a patrol of dark elves, I was pretty sure that it was loud enough they ought to be able to hear it.

I waited, watching the patrol get farther away and smaller again in Sen's vision. I didn't move at first, stunned the cloaks had worked.

We waited until the dark elves were gone from sight before I lowered my hood and made it clear we were safe. I didn't move, reaching out with my mind first.

"They're not permanent solutions," Minsheng said as he helped me back to my feet. "But I'm sure they'll work for a while."

He was right. I hoped that the cloaks held out against whatever we needed them for. They were for now, and it gave me some confidence that we could make it past this road and on to whatever other obstacles might lie between us and the elves we sought.

We trudged on, getting to the road for the first time. I felt grateful that we had those who could create tools to solve problems that came our way so swiftly. Although a part of me wanted to explore this planet and everything on it, we didn't have that luxury. It wasn't a safe zone.

After we'd gone several hundred yards down the road and I obsessed about checking for the next patrol, I realized that I was so tense my shoulders and back were suffering. On top of that, I'd gritted my teeth. I'd never been in enemy territory that was like this.

I had been in the mountain in Mexico, but the cult had been a known source of fear. I'd conversed with some of them without feeling as if my life were in danger. They'd attempted to kill me only once. It didn't feel as if personality clashes were a threat here.

Being on this planet was a different matter. I'd gotten the impression that the dark elf would gladly see me dead and my bonded mythicals stripped of their power and left to rot. That vision added to the fear and kept me on edge. I was pretty sure I wasn't the only one. Rick and Frank were on edge too, though they were used to such trips.

The road wound on for several miles, and we had to step off twice to hide under our cloaks and let patrols pass. Each time, I expected to be revealed or have someone miss something or make a sound at the wrong moment. The next two encounters with patrols passed uneventfully, however.

We'd been trekking along the road for an hour or so. I was trying to decide if we'd gone past a marker or milestone for the next leg of our journey or if this was still the right direction when another patrol came up. The other patrols had come from one direction, but this one surprised me and appeared ahead.

I could have kicked myself as I noticed them too late to do anything about most of our group. Some managed to melt away from the main group to hide out of view of the elves. Too many of us were still out in the open.

I considered running, but that wasn't going to work either. If this patrol group got back to their base and told someone, then we would be in serious trouble. The whole mission relied on us hiding the portal we'd opened. That meant not being seen and not having our presence reported back to anyone.

Of course, that meant detaining anyone who saw us. It

would eventually draw attention to where we were, but that was still easier than having a definite report.

What do you want to do? Zephyr asked as he pulled his cloak hood up again and moved to the side of the road.

I hesitated a moment longer, feeling the air elf ahead mentally reach out and around us, noticing us.

There's no point in hiding. Attack. Take them prisoner. Maybe they can tell us something useful.

Zephyr didn't hesitate to grab more of the earth as we rushed forward, using the air to propel us toward the patrol. Everyone around me was trained in battle well enough to understand what we were doing and prepared to attack as well.

All the soldiers dropped behind rocks and bushes as they pulled out guns. The elementals fanned out, control streaming out from them.

Although I ran forward, the patrol was close enough that I could reach beyond them into the air on the other side. I fought the air elf for control of a section behind them, holding it steady and creating a barrier that would keep them from running that way.

The air elf was overwhelmed in moments, no match for the power and precision I could wield, but that didn't stop the group from throwing everything they had at us. Seth blocked a fireball aimed at me. I saw Cherisse battling for a jet of water, droplets flying in all directions.

Roth ran in front of me when some of it flew my way, absorbing it but not doing anything with it. Then the soldiers and Minsheng opened fire. I helped direct their darts, but the earth below me shook hard enough that I wobbled.

I rose into the air as Zephyr resumed control. The patrol sank into the ground a foot, pinned in place. I then stilled the air, and the soldiers fired again.

All but two of the elves were hit enough times that they fell unconscious. One of the earth elves wearing thick armor and an air elf next to him managed to get loose and hold a barrier around themselves well enough that none of the darts got through.

I blasted them with air, but the air elf had a tight pocket around them, and I struggled to get control of it.

They ran, one of them reached for something on the belt he wore. I didn't know what it was, but Cherisse yelled and tried to blow it out of his hand with water. Knowing that whatever she thought was bad couldn't be good, I blasted the hand with air again, but it wasn't enough.

He fought our elemental attacks, diffusing them and bringing his cupped hand closer to his face. I could see the crackle and feel energy flowing across his armor and knew it was blocking our attacks, which I hadn't bargained for. It was also dart-proof, several projectiles sticking out of it and doing the wearer no harm.

Panicking, I flew at him to tackle him.

Suck the air out of him so he can't talk, Zephyr said. *It's a communication device. We need to knock him out.*

What if I kill him? I replied, doing it anyway.

I reached into his lungs, pain flaring in my head as I pushed past the armor. Holding on, I sucked the air out. The dark elf's hand went to his throat, his eyes wide. I doubled over, pain tearing through my body. Sen, Roth, and Nuri were struggling as well, but I didn't let go.

We couldn't let this elf tell anyone we were here.

I wasn't sure how far to go, but the elf kept trying to lift his arm despite the major running toward him, intent on tackling him now that I couldn't. The elemental elves threw everything they had at the hand and equipment, but nothing was getting through or doing more than making the armor crackle.

The lack of air in the elf's lungs eventually led to him turning a strange shade as his legs buckled. He dropped the device as the major reached him. I let go, but the elf collapsed, eyes wide. He didn't move again. The pain I'd experienced faded, but I shook as I collapsed, not sure I had any energy left.

Sen bounded up to me as Nuri hopped closer, and a weary Roth clopped to my side.

That hurt, Zephyr said.

I killed him, didn't I? I asked as Sen dived into my arms and hugged me.

Cuddling the myconid to me and knowing my mythicals had felt my pain, I waited as everyone else dealt with the aftermath.

Once more, I'd had to kill someone to stop bad things from happening. Shame and disgust flared. I never wanted to kill anyone. I wanted to keep myself and everyone I cared about alive.

CHAPTER NINE

Half an hour later, I was on my feet again. I'd eaten, and the soldiers had buried the elf we'd killed on the road. It hadn't been easy, but an earth elf had helped. Minsheng had stripped the elven patrol commander of the strange armor he wore and begun studying it.

The dark elves we'd knocked unconscious were tied up and off to one side of the road in case another patrol came.

I still felt sick and awful, but Cherisse had come to stand beside me.

"Battle sucks," she said. "And taking a life even more. You're still sensitive to it, and in a lot of ways, you should be grateful for that. My predecessors warned me that I shouldn't let it get too easy. But equally, to understand that sometimes it was necessary. It doesn't make you a bad person to kill. It makes you a bad person to kill without good reason, remorse, and a desire to try not to."

"I don't know if we could have done it another way," I replied, hearing the whine in my voice and not liking it.

"No. You can't know for sure. You had to stop him and

stop him you did. Because more elves and humans and mythicals will die if he discovers that portal. And that's on our side. We might never get to rescue any of these elves we're here for. It's a shit decision to have to make, but you've got to make it, and you did. Now move on and make his death mean something. If you bottle it, it will have been for nothing. If you get this mission done, then it was necessary. Just like a death on our side would be."

I blinked, having never thought about it like that. It was a slippery slope to be too arrogant about it. I wasn't sure I wanted to think about deaths as valid or not. Any death before old age and time claimed a person was a waste.

But she did have a point. I had to continue, and we had to decide what to do with our prisoners and the equipment we'd discovered. Although I wobbled, lightheaded as I got to my feet, I felt better for resting and knew I needed to keep on and get us somewhere safer.

Minsheng came over to me as soon as he noticed me on my feet again, holding out the breastplate and arm guards that had formed the armor.

"This is fascinating tech," he said. "It's inscribed with runes, and they worked small crystals into the fabric."

"And it absorbs and blocks elemental energy?" I asked, pretty sure it had drained me. It had also hurt.

"Pretty much. It's holding a lot of energy. It is worth one of us putting it on. Someone who can make use of it."

Zephyr, you can handle it, I said without hesitation.

He didn't respond at first, staring at the armor, but eventually, he nodded and reached out for it. Minsheng helped him put it on underneath his cloak. It wasn't a perfect fit since the elf had been taller and thinner than

Zephyr, but the straps were adjustable, and I saw Zephyr shift his human form to be a fraction taller.

It made me smirk, but his eyes went wide.

There's a lot of power in this, Zephyr said. *All the elements. It stored all the attacks we threw at it.*

Then feel free to use it, I replied. I had the helmet, and it contained a fair amount of energy, but it wasn't close to full capacity.

"What are we going to do with the prisoners?" the major asked as he came up. His soldiers hung back. Only Rick and Frank looked at ease, having been on several missions with me now.

"I want to find out if they know anything useful, but I want to keep moving," I replied. "Is there any way we can drag them or carry them off the road with us so they won't be detected?"

I could carry two, Roth offered. *We're not moving fast, and the terrain is easier underfoot.*

"We can construct a medical stretcher to carry between my four men, but I wouldn't want to carry more than one."

Looking over the five living dark elves from the patrol, I considered what to do with the other two. I couldn't spare any people to take two back through the portal, and I couldn't leave them here alive to walk away. They'd talk. We could only easily carry three without using elemental power.

"I'll carry the rest," I said. It would drain my power, but I couldn't countenance the alternative.

Let me take over keeping us safe, then, Zephyr said.

I didn't argue with him as the soldiers put together the stretcher, and I helped him get two onto Roth's back. We strapped them in place, then I checked that Roth was okay. I couldn't feel any pain coming from him, but that didn't mean he could bear their weight.

With no better alternative, however, we moved out, taking the five dark elves with us. It wasn't easy to keep two people floating in the air, especially when I felt drained, but I wasn't going to leave them there to die or get away.

We plodded on, letting Zephyr lead us, and kept our party off to one side of the road. We were on the other side from the portal, trudging through the land with no real idea where we were heading. It didn't make anyone feel like rushing.

We kept moving, waiting for the dark elves to wake up, and the terrain changed. Hills rose ahead of us, the ground was rockier and less sandy, and the plant life was less stunted and greener. It wasn't long before there were patches of moss, and I could hear a stream burbling.

It wasn't much, but it was helping keep the area alive. We gravitated toward the water, the path coming closer to it as well. Two hours into the trek, I told everyone to take another break. Cherisse checked the water for us as Zephyr guarded and monitored the road.

Another patrol had passed us. We moved a few yards away to avoid detection, but it was quiet, and the sun was sinking lower. I had no idea how long the days were on this planet, but the walk and area had been hot. I wouldn't be surprised if we were more sunburned than we'd have liked. Having the cooler evening temperatures would be a blessing as we continued.

The water wasn't clean, having several pollutants in it,

but Cherisse and Roth were sure they could filter it. We filled our waterskins. It wasn't ideal, but we'd been here longer than I had expected, and I still hadn't seen the next milestone the refugees had described. They'd talked about hills and a fork in the path and that we needed to take the right-hand turn but stay on the left side until we reached a ruined mossy building.

I'd hoped we'd have already found it, but who knew what it was going to take to get there?

No one else was complaining as we ate and then packed up. We'd signed up for this mission, knowing that it was full of unknowns and danger. It was what it was.

Zephyr continued to lead the way, giving me time to think and process. I wasn't entirely happy with what had happened so far. The death was still weighing on my mind, and the look on the elf's face was one I was trying to shake, but I was determined not to let it make me freeze, as Cherisse had hinted at.

And she was right. The last time I'd killed someone, it had made me nervous in battle. I'd hesitated, and we'd fared badly because of it. For the sake of everyone around me, I had to pull myself together. But it wasn't always that easy.

You're doing what you need to, Zephyr said.

And we still believe in you, Roth added.

The greats also struggled with similar thoughts. Nuri landed on my shoulder again and nuzzled against my ear. He was getting bigger and heavier, and I enjoyed the presence beside me. I was pretty sure that if Sen weren't scouting, she'd have been on the other shoulder and comforting me as well.

I felt better. If the four great elves who had seemingly set some of this in motion had also wrestled with these sorts of questions, then it made me feel less alone. Even Cherisse had helped in her no-nonsense, unapologetic manner.

As we came across the next patrol, we hid again, but I noticed this one was warier. They lingered longer when they were coming past us, seeming to almost pick up on an anomaly on the horizon and one of them took a few steps in our direction.

Hoping that they took no more, I held my breath. The dark elves we'd taken weren't awake yet and had been moved further from the path, but none of them had the cloaks the rest of us were using to hide. I was pretty sure that this group was aware another patrol had gone missing. They were a lot more cautious, communicating and checking things out more meticulously.

I was relieved when the dark elf finally stepped back and jogged to catch up with the rest of his patrol. I untensed muscles that had grown tight while I crouched and hoped that was the last of it for a while.

I watched them leave, Zephyr at my side. Only then did we dare move again.

I could feel Roth growing tired, and a dull ache crept across our bond. I called a halt near the stream, although it had shrunk as we moved closer to the source. I let the others think it was a normal break as I went to Roth's side.

He looked tired, and I was pretty sure he didn't have much capacity left. Without asking, I undid the straps holding the dark elves he was burdened with in place and used my abilities to lower them to the floor.

Giving Roth a gentle stroke, I leaned into him. I was also tired from carrying the other two elves. We would have to wait until they woke up and find out what they knew.

Taking my refilled waterskin, I moved to the dark elf who had been hit with fewer darts and chucked it over his head. He coughed and spluttered and stirred.

"Wake up," I said as I prodded him with my foot and took control of the elements around him.

I wasn't going to let this dark elf escape or do anything I didn't want him to. To be on the safe side, I also created a bubble around us to keep in sound.

It looked as if the elf was going to do nothing but blink and stare around him, but eventually, his eyes fixed on me as he tried to lift a hand and wipe the water off his face. With his hands tied in front of him and bound to his feet by a length of rope, he couldn't get his hands very high, but it made him realize the seriousness of his situation.

"Do you speak Common?" I asked, not sure he would understand me. This was the first time I'd talked to one of the dark elves, let alone interrogated one.

"I do," the guy replied with a slight accent. "Are you her?"

"If you mean Henera, then yes."

"No. He is Henera. She... You are not."

I lifted an eyebrow, wondering if I'd missed something. I wanted to find out what he meant but didn't want to get off-topic.

"I want to ask you some questions. I'm looking for a ruined village in that direction," I said, pointing in the rough direction the refugees had described to us.

The dark elf blinked but didn't respond.

"Do you know where it is?" I asked.

"Possibly. There are many ruined villages. Many old places. The elves here are fewer in number than before. All serve the Henera or perish."

"Right. The Henera is Kirdash?" I asked.

The dark elf flinched, and everyone around me did the same.

"That is a name we shouldn't use."

"Great. Well, I don't serve him, and I haven't perished. What I am is losing my patience, however. I need to find some elves, I need some answers to some questions, and I need to get moving again. You're going to help me, or you're going to wish you had."

He laughed, not intimidated by me.

"You are not Henera. You don't scare me."

"I'm pretty sure that the Henera isn't supposed to scare anyone. Good people don't rule by fear."

This made the dark elf pause, his eyes going wider before he stilled again.

"What do you hope to achieve by resisting him?"

"Peace. Freedom. A way of life that means no one goes hungry or is hurting or suffers. One where we can focus on the beauty in the world and live life to the fullest. Not striving every day to protect those we care about or anything but the desires of our hearts."

I spoke without thinking, but I registered the hush when I stopped. It wasn't anything I'd thought about, but ideals came out of me at the push of a button.

"Will you help me?" I asked.

It was clear the elf was considering it, but he looked around again, buying time.

"Where is our commander?" he asked when he saw we had four of his five companions.

"Dead," I replied, not wanting to lie to someone who might be beginning to trust me. "I didn't want to kill him, but he didn't give me as much choice as I'd have liked."

That made the elf frown. Then his eyes fixed on Zephyr, who was wearing the deceased's armor.

"You are not better. You kill and steal what you want."

I sighed, sure that I'd lost my chance to get this dark elf to talk. It seemed he'd also grown bored with being questioned. He started wriggling to get free, and he started a fire nearby. I put it out, but he set a small one on the rope binding his wrists.

Although I put it out swiftly, it weakened the rope, and he pulled his arms apart. Before he could do anything else, shots were fired and the elf fell back, four feathered darts sticking out of his torso.

I was not sure how I felt about the conversation and how it had gone. It was irritating that he'd insulted me, but I'd learned from him. It wouldn't change finding the refugees we were looking for, but it gave me more information about my main enemy and how he thought and operated.

It was progress.

CHAPTER TEN

I'd woken three of the five dark elf patrols and asked them questions before I gave up. None of them told me anything useful, and I was frustrated by their lack of cooperation.

I understood why. They were terrified of the elf in charge, as everyone on this planet was, and it kept them from answering me. However, most of my frustration came from their unwavering belief that I was there to destroy them and take away their home.

It was keeping them from trusting me.

When the third elf was once more out cold and lying back out on the stretcher, I exhaled and got up. I was getting nowhere. The major came to my side a fraction of a second later, and I was pretty sure he felt similar. This wasn't going well.

"We've not got the ammo to keep hitting these five with sedatives. We've got to do something with them or leave them here."

"Something?" I asked, not sure where he was going with his suggestion.

"We can't afford the people to take them back through the portal. We can't take them onward with us while awake. We either leave them, or we have to get rid of the problem."

I gasped as I finally understood what he was suggesting. Killing people simply because they were inconvenient was something that didn't sit well with me.

The alternative is leaving them somewhere so tied up and restrained that they'll probably die anyway, Zephyr said.

Sighing, I tried to think of another possibility, but none came to mind. This wasn't going to happen the way the major and Zephyr were suggesting. I wouldn't allow it. If I stood any chance of making the world a better place, then I had to be above reproach. I had to make sure no one died who didn't need to.

While still thinking about this, the major was close by with a small pistol at the ready and a look that said he was waiting for my permission to use it, the fourth elf woke up.

Stalling for time, I stepped closer and began the interrogation procedure again. Before I could get much out of the elf, he set fire to the ropes around his wrists and tore loose. Although the soldiers fired darts, they went wide, the fifth and final elemental finally breaking free as well and helping to defend them.

I growled and reached for the elements, but not before something strange happened. The fifth elf pulled another device from a pocket and triggered it. There was a loud explosion from where the elf had been standing, and it knocked me backward. Zephyr seemed to catch me, but we tumbled onto the ground, and I felt the sharp pain of one of my mythicals hurting.

Looking around, I spotted that there were bits of shrapnel and other objects that had flown outward from the device the dark elf had carried. The four other elves were dead, scattered and unmoving. Then I realized that the fifth elf was still holding the device that had exploded and caused the damage.

It didn't look like a bomb, and there was a bullet hole in it. The major's gun was in his hand; he'd shot the device.

Not knowing what else to do, I walked away, tears stinging my eyes. The major hadn't killed any of them deliberately. One glance at his face revealed the shock he felt at the explosion, his arm bleeding from being hit with shrapnel.

Zephyr had taken a chunk in the back of one arm. Mine throbbed in unison as I put distance between me and the mess I'd gotten myself into. I felt sick and sad and angry, along with so many feelings I didn't know how to express them.

Slow down, Aella. We need you with us so we can keep everyone safe. Zephyr's words soothed me, but I could hear the tension in them.

I stopped, letting him catch up to me but keeping my distance from everyone else.

He shook as he put an arm around me.

That is going to haunt my dreams for weeks, I said, not sure how to describe my horror.

I know. It will haunt mine as well. Despite what they say, it doesn't get any easier to see that sort of thing.

Sighing, I tried to think about anything else. Like him, his body hurting so badly we all felt it. As soon as I looked at his arm, I saw why. There was a large chunk of metal sticking out of it.

I moved closer to get a better look. His cloak was torn, the shirt underneath as well. Blood had blossomed from the wound, soaking the sleeve of his shirt. I was worried about him.

It's okay. As long as I don't move much, it will be fine.

Can we pull it out and patch you up? I asked.

The medical kit might have something, but I don't want to take it out and bleed out.

What if I held your blood in like I've done for elven medics in the past? I looked at the wound and reached into him with my mind to feel the area.

Zephyr frowned.

How confident are you? I can turn dragon if it goes horribly wrong, but I think we both know I'm needed in this form.

I'm pretty sure I can patch you up, but having Minsheng on hand might be wise.

We glanced at my Shishou. He had encouraged everyone to move farther from the road, minimizing the possibility of being found by another patrol. The soldiers had buried the dead dark elves. Cherisse was standing some distance away from everyone else.

It didn't take a genius to know she struggled with what we were finding and how well this mission was going so far. This wasn't the rescue and recovery of strong but struggling and downtrodden elves we were hoping for.

I was grateful Zephyr was giving me something else to focus on. Minsheng came over, and we told him the plan.

"I'll do what I can to help. I've got some stuff in the

medical kit. I'm no Daisy, but I've had the basic training the organization insisted on."

It was all the persuading Zephyr needed, and he nodded at me. I reached into the wounded area and connected to the elements there, feeling his blood pump around his body and respond to the foreign object inside it.

As I took control of the blood near the shrapnel and did everything I could to hold it in place, Zephyr reached up and yanked out the shard.

I screwed up my face as pain flared in my arm where the shrapnel had left a hole in his. Zephyr grunted and gritted his teeth, but I didn't lose focus and kept doing everything I could to hold his blood in place. Slowly, I did as I'd seen other medic elves do, and starting at the deepest and least damaged part of the wound, I encouraged the cells to reconnect.

It wasn't easy, and it took a lot of concentration to get right, but I worked on the main artery through that section as Zephyr and Minsheng held the wound shut and kept it clean. Minsheng injected Zephyr with a painkiller to allow us to focus on something other than the pain.

He grunted again as I shifted my mental grip.

Sorry, I said, wondering if I should stop.

It's okay. You're doing an amazing job. It feels weird, like someone is tickling me on the inside, but you're repairing the damage before it gets so bad that the body can't do it easily.

Zephyr was trying to be reassuring, but it might not be true, especially since I could still feel the pain this was causing him. I did my best to continue anyway.

When I'd been working on it for almost an hour straight, and I was exhausted from using my abilities, I stopped. The wound was no longer in danger of bleeding out, and it was significantly shallower. However, it was still hurting. I was aware of the same dull throb as I'd had the last time one of us got hurt like this.

Minsheng stepped in at this point, using something that helped numb the area before he stitched the rest up.

I sat down as Cherisse brought me some food. The soldiers were resting against bushes or their packs, covered entirely by cloaks and making sure they weren't a problem if another patrol came.

Grateful for a group of allies with so much foresight, I thought about what we should do next. I munched as I considered taking everyone back again, but it wouldn't be easy. Not only would it be a huge blow to Cherisse's morale, but the general and the President would likely lose some of their faith in me. They were trusting me with this mission and the resources I'd asked for.

I tried not to think about what was going wrong while I ate and recuperated.

By the time Minsheng was done and Zephyr was ready to go on, the sun was almost down. I was starting to wonder if we'd be able to walk much longer or should make camp.

"We should keep on until the light fails, and then, if we have the energy and the dragon can see well enough, keep going. The only way we're going to win this war is if we don't give up when we could easily turn back. We must use every advantage we have and work together." Cherisse didn't take her eyes off me as she spoke, but I got the feeling that her words were as much for the others as for me.

For now, it was enough. If the group was willing to trudge on, I would too.

Zephyr slipped his fingers into mine, and we put one foot in front of the other, and then the other.

Over the next hour, the patrols grew more numerous. Several times we moved farther away from the road and waited. I saw more patrols fanning out, trying to figure out what had happened to their missing comrades.

At some point, they'd find the six who were dead. We had staged them so it was obvious that some force had brought them in the direction we'd gone and then blown them up. I didn't doubt that hearts and minds would be more set against us after witnessing the destruction of a patrol squad.

I couldn't dwell on that either. Instead, I focused on scanning ahead, holding a barrier that kept most of our noise around us, and aiming for the hills while we could still see them.

By the time we had to rely on Zephyr's sight, the patrols had stopped. Nothing shared the road with us mile after mile.

Giving up and heading back or making camp looked like a good idea, but Zephyr kept walking. He was the only one who could see well enough to know we were on the right track. We didn't dare turn a flashlight on since it would draw attention from miles away.

When I stumbled for the second time and Zephyr had to catch me and put me back up on my feet, I decided enough was enough. I opened my mouth to suggest we camp for the night when a light twinkled in the distance before vanishing again.

I stopped and whispered for everyone else to do the same. In the dark, we'd bunched up to keep from losing anyone, everyone connecting physically to someone else or one of my mythicals or me. My bond with my mythicals made it easy not to lose them, but everyone else needed some way to ground their location.

We watched for a couple of minutes before I was sure I saw the light again. I pointed it out, and as one, we walked toward the source.

It came from an elevated position far away, but it was identifiable as a flaming torch someone was carrying up ahead.

Do you think they're an ally or an enemy? I asked Zephyr when we decided we had to check it out.

No way to be sure, but so far, the patrols haven't been carrying a source of light. They're just keeping the road clear.

True. We haven't seen one for hours.

Even with the missing patrol, they're not looking this far away from where we attacked them, but I suspect they're also not interested in wasting time at night.

I considered replying that I didn't want to waste my time at night either, but I couldn't rest until we'd found out who carried the source of light ahead…or what.

CHAPTER ELEVEN

After another hour, we were close. It was occasionally visible as they walked around what looked like a ruined building.

Now, however, it had disappeared.

We'd gotten close enough that I could make out the outline of the ruins without the light or any other aid, but we were not close enough to detect the torchbearer before they killed their light source.

Let's find one of these with better shelter and walls and camp for the night, I said to Zephyr, not wanting to begin a wild goose chase in the dark if whoever it was had left.

If it came with pizza, a large, comfy bed, and a hot shower, I'd be willing to forgive this place for everything we've gone through to get here.

You and me both. Alas, I fear the dark elf ruling these lands long ago demolished the pizza ovens. His most terrible act. We will have to make do without pizza.

Then I shall not rest until I restore this land and the pizza ovens and pizzas are made under this sun once more. Or these stars.

I chuckled quietly and trudged on. We were two steps into the large, central space of the first ruin when I felt something sharp at my neck. A large presence was wielding it.

"Hi," I said quietly as more people appeared, most of them holding bows and aiming arrows at my team.

"This is our land. We deal with trespassers in the strictest manner. You've got one chance to go back the way you came and leave us."

"I'm sorry," I said, speaking quietly, not wanting to test the blade held at my throat or any other facet of this situation. "We're not aware of who's running what part of this planet, but I'm from Earth, and we've come here at the request of a slave elf in the dark elf's service. My friends and I want to help those in need and cause no other trouble."

"Truly? She sent you to aid us? It worked? The Henera exists?"

"If I understand things correctly, I am the Henera," I replied, the excitement in the man's voice making me less wary of the blade at my throat.

"She's the Henera," Cherisse confirmed from behind me. "And I'm the high tenet. We're here to find the oppressed elves and reunite everyone according to the great prophecy. We'll die defending our right to live a free life, so if you know what's good for you, I'd remove that blade from her neck before someone ends you where you stand."

I'd only heard Cherisse threaten me, and I'd never given

in to her demands when she'd spoken like that, but her words had a strong impact on the elf before us. He removed the blade from my neck, stepped back, and bowed to me.

"Forgive me, Henera. I had no idea. We have hoped for so long in vain that it is hard to know how to act now that it might be happening."

"It's okay. We're all wary and under threat. All of us have walked a hard path to get where we are now, but we're here. I hope I can help. Can you take us somewhere safer so my group and I can rest and figure out how to get you to the nearest safe portal to Earth?"

"Yes, Henera. I would be honored to lead you, although I do not know if we have space for a mighty army or food to feed you all. But those I see with you here would fit within our halls."

"I only have those you see," I replied, hoping to put the man at ease as he got to his feet.

Instead, he looked horrified as he glanced at the small group.

"Don't worry. None of them will hurt you," I added when he gulped and looked at me again.

"Your army. You do have an army, do you not?"

"Not exactly. I didn't bring one here, but there are more elves, mythicals, and soldiers on the other side of the portal. I've come with my best to bring your sick and injured elves to safety so they can heal and recover. We're more than strong enough to achieve that."

The man hesitated again, but after studying my face, he nodded.

"As you wish. I will trust the Henera, but others may wish to see your power displayed to be convinced."

"After food and rest, I will oblige those who have lost hope." I smiled, hoping this would be the end of this strange conversation.

The man ushered us after him. We had to tread carefully and slowly in the dark. He was very practiced at walking among the ruins and had no trouble navigating to the end of a block of buildings. Several times my group members stumbled, which made me wish that I could help them.

All I could do, however, was keep walking and keep my hand on Zephyr and another on Minsheng's shoulder. I could feel Roth, Nuri, and Sen with the soldiers, or in Roth's case, with two. That left Cherisse, Seth, the major, and Ronan stumbling after everyone else and trying not to lose us.

Ronan could also see fairly well, and he was guiding the major and Seth, who had a lot of respect for the centaur. Cherisse walked alone, insisting on being independent. Part of me wanted to encourage her to be less stubborn, but she was also someone you couldn't argue with.

It felt like we picked our way through building after building, going around in circles and through and back again as we made a path through the village. I strongly suspected this was our host's way of being cautious. He didn't have much reason to trust us until I had proved to be Henera. Making it hard to find his home and the vulnerable people living in it was understandable.

When we did finally reach a ruin with a roof over one

section, my feet were aching, and I was so tired and hungry I was barely able to keep going.

We followed him in, out of the view of anyone watching, then stopped. I thought we'd been tricked when two elves jumped down from the rafters, having concealed themselves until we came close. They held weapons, and they reached for the air and earth.

Without hesitation, I took control of those elements, holding them and blocking anyone else from doing so. It was an aggressive move, but I wasn't going to let myself be put in danger again. It was bad enough that I'd let someone get close enough to hold a blade to my neck.

The three elves conversed in Elvish, but they spoke rapidly and had an accent that made it hard to understand. I heard them mutter something about Henera a few times, and the two new elves looked me over.

I considered showing off, but I had no idea what was going on or if it would make things worse. I still didn't know what to do when one of them moved to the back of the building.

He let out a strange whistle, then the ground moved, letting in some light and revealing the head of a person carrying another flickering torch. I was close enough to see that there were steps leading down. Wherever we were going next, it was underground.

It would be impossible for Roth and Ronan to get down there, which bothered me. Steps weren't easy for large four-legged creatures.

I'll stay up here with them, Zephyr said. *Take Sen, Minsheng, the major, and Cherisse with you. There's no point in the rest of us going down into the tight space, and I'm still not sure we're safe up here.*

I wanted to argue with him, but he had made a good suggestion. We still didn't know what this was and if these people were friendly. It wouldn't be wise to take everyone underground even if we could fit.

Trying not to show my fear or paranoia about what was coming, I stepped forward and bowed to the elf in the hatch.

"Good evening," I said, not sure what time it was. "I hope you don't mind the intrusion. We're here to help. Can I come down with a few of my friends so we can figure out what might be done?"

The man blinked, then looked at the first elf I'd met.

"Let her come down," he said in Common.

I didn't think the elf was going to listen since his broad body continued to block the opening, but eventually, he nodded and moved back.

I stepped closer, determined to be the first to walk confidently into this situation. If this was the dark elf's strategy to trick me, I wasn't afraid. Whatever happened, I had to save people, especially if we were going to be killing others. I didn't want to kill anyone, but if it happened while I was trying to save the ones I could, it would help.

The steps were steeper than I feared, and I had to turn around to descend. I pulled an air barrier tight around me, grateful I was able to control the elements. At the same time, I reached out and connected with more air and the earth. I could feel the markers of many different elves, but no one was currently using magic.

Minsheng followed me into a dark passage. It also

sloped down, heading under the ruins above and making it harder to figure out where we were going.

I heard some of the others follow, but the guy with me motioned for me to walk down a hall. It was dark and narrow, but someone had lit a torch at the far end, and the light spilled toward me. When we were on the dirt path, the elf at the door shut it and came to guide me.

"This way," he said as if there were an alternative and we had to pick an option.

I tried to still my racing heart as I wondered what was in store down here, but I wasn't going to have to wait long to find out. The corridor was short, and they hurried us down it.

When I came around the corner, it was my turn to hesitate and stare. Under the ruins of a town was another town, hewn from the native rock and dug into the dirt. It had a stream running down the center of it, but more importantly, there were about a hundred elves, mythical creatures, and members of other races present.

Most of them were very old, very young, or injured.

No one noticed I was there, and I watched as they went about their lives. Minsheng came far enough around the corner that he could see what had made me pause.

He let out a low whistle. This was a lot of people to rescue, especially when I only had a team of fourteen, and four of those were mythicals. I hadn't expected this.

Finally, they spotted me. The elf with me didn't give me much choice but to move into the light of the edge of the cavern. There were whispers, and a strange hush rippled out from the person who had first noticed me.

I didn't say anything, still wondering how we'd rescue

so many people or get this many injured to the portal. The whole thing hinged on them accepting that leaving was better.

It was obvious why the men who had let me in were so surprised that there were few people on my team. There weren't enough of us, not even close. We didn't have the medical supplies to help everyone who needed it. Too many were hobbling, injured, malnourished, or simply exhausted for us to get them to the portal quickly.

And all of them were staring at me.

You should say something, Zephyr said, following what I could see. *They look as if they could do with the hope having the Henera around will bring.*

But they don't know me. I might be the Henera, but for what I can offer them, I might as well be just another elf or refugee.

That's not true, and you know it. Trust yourself. Trust what you're capable of and what's in your heart.

I exhaled, not sure I knew anything for sure, but I was willing to try to give the elves before me hope. Hope was powerful. Sometimes it was all people needed.

They shifted, and someone coughed. I was running out of time, so I stepped to the edge of the ledge I was on.

"Hello, everyone. I know none of you have ever met or heard of me, but I'm an elf from Earth. I and my bonded mythicals opened a portal and came through to aid you as best we can after conversing with one of your allies in the dark elf's palace. I don't know how best I can help, but I have brought some of my strongest allies with me. We have medical supplies with us."

I stopped speaking, not sure I was doing a good job, but one cheered and then another. They were looking at me with hope-filled faces, and the man with me was trying to quiet them.

Within seconds, they fell silent.

"Please, everyone, go about your day, and we'll discuss what is best. There is much to learn and figure out, and I know you will have many questions."

I exhaled as someone else became the center of attention. My emotions had been jerked around and sent in directions I had not expected today. There was little left for me to be a leader.

CHAPTER TWELVE

When I finished my final energy bar and sat back, the man in front of me, Aolis, motioned for me to take the cup he held out. While we'd opted not to accept any food from this little underground community, sharing a drink was a sign of trust and friendship.

I took a mouthful and handed it to Minsheng. He did the same. Before long, everyone had swallowed some of the spiced fruit drink. It made me think of a Christmas beverage, but it was alcoholic. I was grateful that they only expected us to take a single swig.

"Your presence here is an honor. Please, tell us what you know and what you think you can do to aid us," Aolis requested.

"It is an honor to be among you," I replied, hoping I was being respectful enough.

Over the next hour, I explained who I was and what I was capable of and briefly went through the events that had led me through the portal to them.

When I spoke about connecting with the dark elf and

fending him off, Aolis' eyes went wide, but he didn't interrupt me.

By the time I was done talking, and Aolis had asked his questions about my emotional and physical journey to this point, I was exhausted. It was late, and we had traveled all day.

"You are welcome to sleep here for as long as you need, but I must ask before you do. What do you intend to do with us? I am no fool, and I know you have intentions. You would not give up everything you have on your planet to come here and face the dark elf without the portal muting his powers if you did not have to."

"My initial hope was to offer you a new home on my planet in the elven communities we have there. Somewhere everyone can rest and recover, and one day be able to rescue more elves and free everyone."

As I said the last part, I realized it was true, but instead of reacting positively to my words, Aolis frowned.

"That will be no easy task. Everyone here is frail or sick. They have short young legs or old tired ones. How do you propose that so many who cannot defend easily will be able not only to endure traveling such a distance but do so while patrols regularly move along the main road to it?"

"I won't lie; it's not going to be easy, but I hope we can come up with a way to help your people make the journey and keep you safe. While I will try to avoid the patrols, we can handle them if we need to." I thought back to our fight with the patrol that had spotted us and how the armor the commander had worn had made it much more difficult. It wasn't ideal to make it sound as if we'd coped better than we had, but we were getting better all the time as well.

"This is good news in some ways, but not so much in others. I am grateful you do not try to make light of this and say it will be easy, but I think you did not expect so many of us."

"We didn't," I replied, willing to confess that. "But that doesn't mean we can't accommodate you all. It might mean we need a better plan to get you to the portal, and any help from elves who can control the elements would be very much appreciated."

This made him think, and he looked at the elves around him.

"There are some here who can help, but not many. We are not taught to use our abilities as it sounds like you have been. I do not think any of us have ever used them in combat. We are not the elves bred for this sort of thing, but we do wish to be somewhere safer. We also wish to live above ground once more. Most of all, we wish to see this land free."

"Then we can help. We will figure out the best way to get you through the portal, even if it takes all night."

Aolis nodded, called for more drink, and invited a couple of other men to sit with us. It took me by surprise, his wariness changing to enthusiasm before I could blink, but I could feel and hear the hope in his voice as he asked me to tell these new men what we had on the other side of the portal.

Although I kept it brief, they were interested in a new life. Minsheng interjected after a few minutes, however, and steered us back to the main task: getting everyone to the portal.

It took another two hours to formulate a plan everyone

agreed on. We would leave together. We needed Zephyr in dragon form and Sen to scout, and I needed to give us early warning of patrols.

Even without planning, it was apparent we were operating on faith and hoping nothing would make the patrols more aggressive or hesitant or cause them to deviate from the roads. Given that we'd killed an entire patrol on our way here, there was a chance that the following day would bring an entirely new problem.

When Aolis was satisfied enough to nod, I finally relaxed. I was exhausted in a whole new way. We had a plan, and while it wasn't perfect, it was better than no plan.

I got up since it appeared we were done.

"Is there anywhere our party could rest?" Minsheng asked before I could speak. "We have come a long way in a short period of time and would benefit from a few hours' sleep before we escort everyone to the portal."

Aolis nodded and motioned for the man beside him.

"Greltar, show them to the larger emergency room," he said before turning back to us. "It's one room and not the most comfortable, but we have a lot of people here, and it's not likely to be needed before morning."

I wanted to ask how often they needed the emergency room, but something held me back. Part of me didn't want to know. It wasn't going to change anything or help me rest. It wasn't going to make any difference to what we did after I awoke. Instead, I asked about the mythicals we'd left on the surface.

"We can take them to an underground enclosure with easier access. Do not fear for them. We won't let them be detected."

That was what I needed to hear, and Zephyr sent a wave of reassurance. Stifling a yawn, I allowed them to lead me back to the main area. It was still bustling and many were off in one corner, tending to what appeared to be a small farm.

The emergency room was just that, a large room with hospital beds and tools. It was clean but had poor lighting, and there was no sign of medication or anything to treat any illnesses. These elves were doing what they could with what they had, but it wasn't much.

Elves pushed aside the equipment. Most of it was strange, but some of it was similar enough to Earth-based tools that I had an idea of what it was for. Once there was a clear floor space, straw-filled mattresses were fetched and laid out for us, as well as thin blankets.

I didn't take one since there weren't enough for everyone. Instead, I opted to lie close to a wall and snuggle under a jacket. It was strange to be surrounded by the soldiers and elves, but I was so exhausted I was soon asleep.

Minsheng woke me a short while later. My head was pounding and my mouth was dry. I yawned and stretched, not sure when I'd last had anything to drink but aware that getting water was likely to be hard. We'd replenished our water bottles when we could, but we had not wanted to drain anyone's ability, and this underground village was very dry.

Cherisse has gone to look for a water source, and she took Roth with her, Zephyr told me as Minsheng helped me to my feet. *They don't have much here and are wary of using it for traveling.*

They're worried we can't get them to safety?

Wouldn't you be? They barely know us, and they don't know what we're capable of, only that the patrols could kill most of them.

True. I sighed. This wasn't going to be easy, but we'd promised to help them, and it was necessary.

When I emerged from the building, Aolis spotted me and came over.

"Our village is as ready as it is going to be to leave. We are bringing only what is dear to us or needed to sustain us on this journey. There is still strength in our people, but the young and old will not manage a great speed."

"We can ask no more of you than your best. We will do everything we can to ease the strain of this journey and get your people to safety. There is a much better life waiting for them on the other side. Food, water, and homes. Medicine, and other elves who will aid them in learning how to use the elements better than they do now."

That comforted Aolis. He took my hand and patted the back of it.

"It has been a long time since we had hope. Many come here to die, and peace is all we can offer them."

I had no idea how to respond to his statement other than to feel we were doing the right thing. This was no way for anyone to live.

As soon as Cherisse returned, Roth having filled himself with water, I went over to them. Cherisse and I used our powers to drain the water from the pegasus. We filled every container we had as well as some from the village, while the water elf told me how they had modified the entrance and exit to the underground dwelling to accommodate the centaur and the pegasus.

The nearest elves marveled at what we were doing, and a couple of young children came over to stroke the pegasus. Roth basked in the attention as we passed what he'd fetched. We went over the plan one last time.

Roth would bring up the rear, along with Minsheng, Ronan, and Cherisse. Their powers and skills were suited to helping the people move rather than fighting in a desert. Roth and Ronan had agreed to carry one of the worst injured elderly and some of the smaller children. Minsheng and the soldiers were going to carry others, and I picked up a mother's pack so she could carry her baby.

We moved to the surface with everyone else, the stronger male elves carrying the injured and infirm. Zephyr transformed into a dragon. There were gasps from those who saw it. The sun was coming up, and it glinted off his shiny scales.

We loaded those who could not walk onto his back. There were four of them, the largest number he'd ever carried for an extended period. Once we had secured them in place, he looked at me.

I can take another. They're so frail and underfed that they're lighter than I was expecting.

Are you sure? I asked, not sure I wanted to burden him further, even if he thought he could handle it.

Yes. Let us make this easy on their feet. I can carry another and still fly.

I passed the information to Aolis and he selected an elderly male elf. The man was walking relatively well but was unburdened and stooped enough that he'd be one of the slowest.

Everyone else had to walk. I surveyed the growing group of elves. They were scared and huddled together, but they were also bright-eyed and willing. We would walk slower than I'd like, but it was time to move out.

No sooner had I thought that than Zephyr spread his wings and took to the air. It was the signal everyone had waited for. I moved to the front with Nuri on my shoulder and the major and Seth at my sides. The soldiers mingled with the column, along with any stronger elves who had skill in combat.

Once everyone was in place, I felt the air. I wanted to form a barrier around us all, but there were too many—over a hundred elves and children in the column behind me, four abreast. I couldn't encase that many and still reach out far enough to keep us safe.

Nuri also rose into the air, intending to fly high enough that he would be difficult to spot and let me know if he saw movement. He was also going to guide us on the most efficient route back. Zephyr would fly much lower, barely above the ground and off to one side, limiting his likelihood of being seen by patrols.

Without further delay, we left, Sen bounding off within seconds to scout ahead.

The tug in my stomach at being separated from my mythicals was almost too much to bear, but it was necessary. I could use the bond to know where to go and if I should go faster or slower. Roth was moving at the pace of the slowest in our small caravan.

The patrols had passed frequently the day before, so I

was sure we would face one before too long. The question of when and how many before we had everyone safe lingered in my mind. We'd spent most of a day traveling to get here, and we couldn't move as fast on the way back.

Still, we could try to make it before nightfall.

CHAPTER THIRTEEN

We were an hour in, and some of the more elderly and injured were beginning to slow their pace when Sen stopped and tucked herself behind a bush. I focused on what she could see and noticed the kicked-up dust and the glint of sunshine on armor that indicated a patrol was on the way.

Without hesitation, I lifted my arm and gave the signal. As one, the group turned to the side of the road and hurried into the desert. There was no way for us to hide this many elves in plain sight. I stayed where I was to make sure they were safe.

Zephyr flew down, leading the way. The elves, soldiers, and everyone else with a cloak brought up the rear. I slowly formed a wall of air, then made it colder. As everyone retreated, I backed up with the wall and left the roadway.

Sen stayed where she was, and the distance between the myconid and me grew. It hurt by the time I thought everyone was far enough back.

The patrol was almost on top of her, so she didn't dare move. I continued pulling back the barrier, placing it in front of the refugees but behind our team of elves and soldiers.

As one, we hunkered down under our cloaks. The elves behind us gasped, no longer able to see us, including the children the soldiers had been carrying.

"It's okay. They're still here. They'll keep us safe," Zephyr said a moment later, his deep voice rumbling across the desert.

I wasn't sure they believed him, but they stayed put and waited. That was all we needed them to do.

It wasn't long before a few of the smaller children fussed, however, not enjoying being in the heat of the day without knowing why they were no longer moving. Not sure what else to do as the patrol came closer, Sen followed them at a safe distance to show me where they were. I added sound dampening to the barrier I'd created.

Although it wasn't perfect, it would help keep any noise we made from reaching the patrol. We had to see if they would move past us without noticing we were there. We were as hidden as we could be; Sen couldn't see us when she glanced our way, the elves behind something and the barrier I had created and the cloaks hiding the rest of us.

I still couldn't breathe properly, my heart hammering in my chest as the patrol marched toward us. There was one armored elf again, no doubt the strongest person in the squad. They were marching at a steady pace. Every few yards, they looked around.

Every part of me wanted to reach out and take control of the air. That would let me know they were moving past and were not aware of us, but they would be controlling the elements around them. If I reached beyond my barrier, they would likely discover us.

The wait was excruciating, and it took all my control not to move or say something, especially when the people and mythicals behind me grew restless.

All clear, Sen said when the patrol slipped out of view.

I exhaled, letting the tension leave my body, then I got up and pulled my cloak's hood down. Relief rippled through the elves as I dropped the barrier.

The soldiers and elves on my team got up and encouraged the first of the refugees toward the road. Sen bounded ahead again.

Everyone was slower this time, but they had benefited from the rest, even if it had been strange for many of them. They understood when we reached the road and the fresh footprints of a patrol showed in the dirt on the road.

It was progress, even if it had been tense.

When I drank the water in my bottle, it was warm. I wondered how well this plan was going to work. We had many people with us, and the road was long. The small stream that ran to one side was not big enough, and we would eventually run out of water.

I was also using my abilities more than I had hoped. I hadn't factored in suppressing the noise of small children who couldn't stand in silence for half an hour. Every patrol that came past forced us off the road for a while as we got everyone to a safe distance, waited, and then came back to the easier terrain.

It was going to be a long day.

The combination of the lack of water and the overuse

of my powers had my head hurting when a patrol forced us off the road for the fourth time. The patrols had been few enough that the day was more than half gone, and we had left the stream behind. It had taken my team about four hours to get to this location, the water a good measure of how far we'd come, but it would take this group longer.

Zephyr was tired, Sen was no longer bounding as vigorously, and Nuri was resting on my shoulder. It wasn't ideal.

The major tromped beside me.

"I think we're going to need to let these people rest soon. I know they rest when we hide from a patrol, but that's tense, and they need time to eat," the major said quietly.

I sighed, but he was right. As much as I wanted to get everyone to safety, they needed to be able to keep moving, and that was a lot to ask of someone who was sick or injured.

I'll scout for a place off the path. Somewhere with bushes and rocks for shade, Zephyr said as he veered to the left and nearer the portal side of the road, still flying low.

Since we were tired too, I felt better about the decision, but it was going to put everyone in more danger. Despite my fears, Zephyr found a suitable area. The major led everyone in that direction, with Nuri guiding him.

Once again I stayed near the road, ready to throw up a barrier if needed and defend the group if a patrol spotted them. I couldn't relax, but it was the best I could do. This planet was full of difficulties and dangers, and I wanted to get off it.

Now that I had seen the place, I knew why everyone

wanted to be on Earth, and I'd barely scratched the surface.

The major and the soldiers worked with the hardier elves to hand out what little food we had as I finally made my way after everyone. Sen stayed near the road to spot patrols and give enough warning that I could throw up a noise wall if nothing else.

I felt terrible leaving my myconid on her own and still on duty, but she seemed happy, and I didn't want to make it harder on the rest of us by stopping her. We were in better shape, and we were used to it.

Thankfully, there was enough food that I could eat, and my strength increased as I leaned against Zephyr. It was almost idyllic as he shielded me and others from the sun; the bushes and rocks did the rest. I could feel Roth suffering and looked his way when I felt the first twinge of pain.

The water pegasus had his head down as he walked slowly over to me. In the heat, he had continued to dry up, and his beautiful translucent skin was wrinkled and sagging, especially around his middle and his head.

I reached out to run a hand across it and recoiled since my touch made him hurt.

You need water, I said to Roth.

Yes. Is there anything you can do? I fear I will not make it in this heat without being replenished.

I reached into the soil below me, searching for water to connect to and closing my eyes to concentrate. If Roth was asking me for help, it had gotten bad.

Cherisse merged her mind with mine, then I was in the full sunlight. Zephyr had taken human form and come to stand beside me.

With the three of us combining our power, we could delve deeper. The ground was dry so far down that it took our collective skill and strength to bring up a small amount of water.

It felt as if it took an age. Zephyr and I connected to the earth to create a well-like opening to help the water rush up faster. As it came up, the task got easier, but we lost a little along the way. The ground was so dry it sucked the liquid out of our grasp and refused to give it up.

Our frustration was intense, but the relief Roth felt when we connected him to the water supply was worth every moment.

As he filled out and shone again, an intense sensation came across our bond. Roth basked in it, relaxing and letting it wash over him.

I kept sending, but I soon felt drained again. Cherisse and Zephyr were drained as well.

Eventually, I stopped. Roth looked like his usual self, the colors dancing on his skin, along with the shimmer of water on the inside. He wasn't so full that I would expect him to be able to pump some out at an enemy, but he no longer looked sick or hurt. I hoped he could hold up until we reached the portal. It wasn't a trick we could repeat since it had cost us too much energy.

When I backed up and looked around, the majority of the elves were staring at us. I didn't doubt it was the first time they'd seen elves work together to achieve something like this.

Cherisse didn't stop but reached for one of the largest water containers we had.

I hesitated, wanting to help her since her face looked

strained, but Zephyr placed a hand on my shoulder.

She's a water elf, and we need water. Save your strength for the patrols and getting us to the portal. We will need what you and I have left before this is over.

Despite Zephyr's recommendation, I still wanted to help, but I held back. Instead, I fetched more containers, letting Cherisse exhaust herself to fill them with water.

No sooner had she finished and stepped back than the major and Aolis figured out how much water we had and doled out a third to each of us. Cherisse collapsed as Zephyr morphed into a dragon, shading us from the sun as I helped her sit and drink some water.

There were murmurs of gratitude as those who were mobile came to get water and then sat back down. Cherisse smiled at each of them, softening when so many showed her what her actions meant to them.

I sat beside her and pulled out the last energy bar in my pack. I offered it to her, then Zephyr shifted closer, letting us lean on him in the shade.

"Last one?" she asked.

"Yup, but you need it more."

"Split it," she replied as she took it, broke it in half, and handed me one of the pieces.

I wasn't about to argue with her. Leaders didn't like to put themselves above others, not good ones. We cared for those around us, pushing ourselves to limits others didn't know were reachable. That was why we ended up as leaders: we pushed harder and farther to see if we broke.

I didn't know what to say. This woman had been responsible for some of the most traumatic events of my life, and she'd shown no mercy. She'd been indirectly responsible for the death of a friend, and she had been willing to risk my life to force my dragon to open a portal.

Yet she'd grown, and so had I. Now we were on the same team, making the best of a difficult situation. I knew Cherisse had drawn up the water because she had thought it for the best, yet she'd gone far too far. However, I wanted her at my side.

It was strange to think of someone both positively and negatively. It wouldn't be easy to reconcile what Cherisse had done, but she was trying to save people now. She was using the power she had for good.

Knowing how imperfect I was made me give her the benefit of the doubt and want to help her get back to the right side of this war and stay there.

"Thank you," Cherisse said a few minutes later. It was almost time to get moving again. "You've done what I couldn't."

"We have not done it yet," I replied. "But you've been a big part of it."

"You've gone about it the right way. You've done this with regard for the lives around you and the impact your decisions have. Neither of us is perfect, but you're doing a good job."

"All any of us can do." After standing, I helped her to her feet.

She was struggling, but she did her best to hide it. I wasn't going to draw attention to it if she didn't want me to.

"Let's get this bunch to the portal and prove us both right." I grinned.

She smiled back. That was a plan we could get behind.

CHAPTER FOURTEEN

It took Sen a few minutes to give me the go-ahead. Another patrol had gone past while we stopped. She sensibly waited until it was past us before letting me go forward with the elves.

Although I considered not taking them back to the road and straight toward the portal, there were still a fair few miles to cover, and the surface was firmer and easier to tread on the road. It would also give the refugees a comforting marker to follow. On top of that, there was more cover since trees and bushes lined it.

The portal stood out from the desert like a sore thumb once you got close enough. There was very little in the way of bushes around it. Once we got close, we would have to make the last of the journey in one go, and it would be better if it was close to dark.

In my pack, I had the helmet and a couple of tablets, as well as one of the crystals we'd taken from the dark elves when we'd pushed them out of the mountain in Mexico. The other elves had something similar with instructions to use them only in emergencies. I was aware that several of us were close to needing them.

And there were bound to be more patrols.

I led the way again, getting us back on the road and moving. After a longer rest and food, the group moved faster, giving me hope that it wouldn't be long after dark before we were at the portal and getting these elves to safety. The people on Earth would be worried about us. We hadn't intended to be away for this long.

Nuri send a message? the firebird asked.

I considered it, liking the idea but thinking how it would feel if Nuri went through the portal while I was on this side. It didn't strike me as comfortable for my bond with him, even if it could cope with that.

It might drain your power, Zephyr said when I leaned toward doing it. *But if Nuri went through, dropped off the message, and came right back, it might be worth it. They could meet us on this side with supplies and extra firepower.*

Once again I hesitated, knowing there were merits to the idea and knowing that I was our main line of defense if anything went wrong. I thought about the previous day and how difficult it had been to get past the patrol commander's armor and take him out of the equation. Although I still hoped to avoid fighting any patrols, there was a chance that we wouldn't be so fortunate.

Give it another hour, I thought back, hoping it was the right decision to make. If we were going to request that the soldiers and elves on the other side meet us, there was little point in doing so before we would be ready to meet them. Having a large group on this side of the portal increased the risk of being discovered.

The risks outweighed the benefits.

None of them argued with me or suggested I might be wrong, which let me relax and hope I'd made the right decision. It wasn't always easy to determine the correct course of action, but I was glad we were making progress.

As the sun sank lower, it moved in front of us, making me squint and making it harder for Sen to see what was coming. I grew tenser as the problem got worse, but we avoided another patrol without much difficulty, the group now knowing what they needed to do.

As I brought them back to the road again, I could see that they were very fatigued. They were slower, and many were hobbling, leaning on someone else, or walking along with their heads down and their weak bodies barely lifting one foot after another.

Time to send that letter? Zephyr asked as he slowly circled overhead.

I think so.

I reached into my pack and pulled out paper and a pen. As I walked, I wrote down the basic information the soldiers and elves would need on the other side of the portal and requested that they bring assistance. It wasn't perfect, but it would have to do.

As soon as I had folded it, Nuri flew down and landed on my shoulder. I used a piece of twine to tie it to his leg and hoped it would hold. When the major saw what we were doing, he let out a laugh.

"The general flies birds or something. When we get back, remind me to ask him about getting a message pouch for Nuri and you. Then we can send messages to him without you having to run the risk that they fall off." I nodded but lifted an eyebrow, surprised yet again by the everyday lives of the people I fought with.

Nuri didn't wait around but climbed back into the air and veered toward the portal. I watched him go, feeling the tug in my stomach grow stronger and hoping I could endure whatever happened to our bond when the firebird went through the portal.

I tried not to worry about it. Instead, I focused on the road and the fatigued and bedraggled group of mythicals behind me. They slowed more as Roth came up and told me how slow the slowest were going.

It was frustrating and tense to wait for the ones struggling most to catch up since none of the hardiest were able to walk slowly enough to accommodate their pace anymore. Sen was finding it harder to see with the sun in her face. The dryad was also exhausted.

None of this was going to work for much longer.

Aolis made his way to the front of the group as I was thinking this to tell me something I'd already figured out. I nodded as he approached.

"They're going to need to rest again," he said, looking as if he wanted to cry.

"Let's take them off the road toward the portal and find what shelter we can until nightfall brings us relief," I said, hoping it was the right course of action.

I hoped it wouldn't be long, but the children were getting noisier as they grew hungry and dehydrated, and the elderly were in danger of passing out or giving up entirely. We had to do something now, especially as the patrols were going to be harder to spot.

Aolis was quick to work with the soldiers to encourage

the elves on and away from the road as I stood there once more, holding the line and wishing there was more I could do.

As the last few elves came past, my heart sank farther. They were barely upright, let alone able to make the miles still to go to the portal.

I used the air to help them, lightening their limbs and essentially blowing them along a bit. I could see the gratitude. I didn't stop as I walked behind them despite how much it was draining me, knowing this was the only way to get everyone to safety.

I reached into the bag I carried and felt for the crystal that contained air elemental power. I was going to need it if I wanted to be sure I didn't drain myself. The last thing I wanted to do was break my bonds as Nuri was making his way to and then through the portal.

With the crystal in hand, I used all the power I could from it, barely using my own to power anything while aiding the group I protected.

We were still several hundred yards from the road when Sen panicked and showed me what she could see. The falling sun had obscured a larger patrol group, this one moving slower and kicking up less of a dust cloud and containing two dark elves in body armor.

I gave the signal to the rest of the group, but so many of them were ahead of me rather than behind that I didn't get their attention at first. There was little I could do about getting everyone to hurry up.

Zephyr landed ahead, dropping off the elves on his back and raising the alarm in silence a moment later. Still, it cost us precious time, and I had to decide whether I would help the most infirm of the refugees or put up a barrier to protect them from a fight with the patrol.

I hesitated, caught between two decisions that could be wrong and unsure of which was most important. As I looked at the frail faces and the fear in their eyes, I knew I had to help them away from the danger.

It wasn't ideal, and I ran the risk of not being able to protect them if the patrols attacked first and asked questions later, but I had to hope we'd avoid this one as we had the last few.

The refugees were still limping along as best they could when Sen showed me what she could see once more. It was too late. The patrols had spotted us.

Come back to me, I said to her as Nuri reached the portal, and Roth stopped following the refugees. Zephyr rose back up into the sky in dragon form. We were the first to be aware that it was too late.

I kept the refugees moving as Aolis, the soldiers, Minsheng, Seth, Ronan, and Cherisse reacted to the threat and rushed back to stand near me. Most of the others kept the refugees moving, and I encouraged the major to go with them, but he shook his head as he thrust a spare pistol at me.

"You're not going to stand here and defend this lot alone. They stand a better chance of getting to the portal if we stop this patrol entirely."

Gulping, I didn't try to argue. Instead, I threw up the usual barrier between us and the weakest elves. I wouldn't be able to hold it and fight, but I was going to make sure no one died on my watch again.

I reached into my bag and pulled out my helmet. It was

time to put everything I had left into defending these refugees. I had to get these elves safe and show this patrol that we meant business. I had to make sure that none of the patrol escaped since they'd seen us. They would report in if we didn't stop them and either kill them or take them with us.

I exhaled as I jammed the helmet on, trying not to worry about what it did to my appearance. It wasn't as much for defending as it was for attacking, and I intended to put it to good use.

As soon as I connected to the gemstones embedded in it, I felt their raw power. I'd been filling them every day. Although I'd never filled them completely, they were a welcome boost now.

The patrol came closer, having no idea who I was. Not one of them was hesitant about facing a few elves in the middle of the desert. If I hadn't been defending so many, I'd have grinned, enjoyed the challenge, and showed them the error of their ways. The truth was, I was terrified.

Behind me were more lives than I had ever had to defend with so few fighters. I was down a mythical since Nuri had paused by the entrance to the portal. When Zephyr landed beside me, I felt braver, however. Aolis was wearing the armor Zephyr had taken the previous day, but I wasn't sure he knew how to use it.

Given Zephyr had been in dragon form most of the day, it was best where it was. With any luck, it would help him protect the refugees.

I took control of the elements around us and felt the other elves merge their minds with mine to strengthen my hold. The patrol couldn't hit the refugees or us if they had nothing to work with.

I felt their challenge as they followed suit and merged their control as well. The soldiers opened fire as soon as they were in range, but the air elves had a defense up, and none of the darts hit.

Frowning, I reached for control of that too, but even with the helmet powering me and the help from Zephyr, I couldn't break through.

I strode closer, knowing it would strengthen my attacks, and my allies came with me. It made the barrier behind me harder to keep up, especially when the fire elementals in the patrol found a way to get the projectiles past it. The flames jetted out of the gauntlets on their wrists.

They smacked into the barrier as I pulled on the air gemstone and the tablets I carried to keep my power going. I also worked with the fire elementals to form the beginning of our signature twister.

Now that I controlled fire and heat, they were easier, and we soon had one spinning. Unlike the previous versions, where I started them small and grew them until they could hurt someone, I started this one large, spinning it around us.

It sucked sand into it, blocking out everything else as I let go of the barrier and focused on the vortex and the ground beneath us.

My team moved close to me, allowing Zephyr and me to huddle together. The far wall of the tornado hit the dark elves. Two were sucked into it, unable to keep their feet, but the rest held firm, rooting their feet despite me controlling the earth.

I growled and moved closer to them, my mythicals moving with me. I could tell the dark elementals were beginning to feel the strain, the air bubbles they were holding around the patrol blocking only so much of the flying sand.

Although my twister was slowly overpowering the elves, they were trying to take control of everything and anything. Unlike them, our group wasn't fresh. My head was pounding from the effort of keeping the tornado going and holding off the patrol elves.

We can't keep this up long enough, Zephyr said. *We need to come up with a new plan.*

He was right, but I couldn't think of anything better. We couldn't let these dark elves get away. If they did, they would bring more of Kirdash's followers, which would be bad news. At some point, they would realize this portal was open. If we had more time, we could shut it after we passed through.

Trying to think of another solution, I controlled the descent of the tornado, winding it down. As it faded out and dropped the sand to the desert floor, I realized I could do nothing but hold a barrier and hope. I was exhausted.

CHAPTER FIFTEEN

"We need to hold them in place," Cherisse said as she knocked another one on his back with a water blast. No sooner had she finished than she sagged where she was. Roth leaned toward her, helping hold her up.

It was the sign of weakness the patrol needed. I might have taken out three of their kind with the tornado, but there were still too many of them left. The elves hit back, attacking the elements we held to steal them from us.

Not sure what else to do, I gave up everything but enough air to create a barrier in front of us.

"Retreat," I said, hoping the others would understand for now. It wasn't ideal, but I couldn't see how we could win this fight anymore, and as much as I wanted to protect the portal, we had to protect the lives of the elves we'd persuaded to trust us above keeping the active portal a secret.

That was going to be easier said than done, however. I heard a shout from the other side of the refugees as they spotted another patrol, this one coming from the direction we'd been traveling. They had canine creatures with them, and it was clear they were tracking the refugees.

I tried not to panic, but the refugees did so, scattering as if this was usually what they did.

"This way," Aolis called as they ran, many stumbling or falling.

It was chaos, and no matter what I did, I could only protect a few of the elves. Some came toward the soldiers and me, and we herded them into a group and toward Zephyr as he slipped into dragon form.

Get help, I said to Nuri, feeling the tension between us and aware that it was now or never.

The firebird didn't hesitate, just leaped at the portal. At first, it felt as if someone had torn my stomach out and I doubled over, gasping and clutching my middle.

As I got used to feeling my bond stretch through the portal, it hurt less, but it was still the most uncomfortable feeling I had ever experienced. I narrowly dodged a firebolt supposed to burn me to a crisp before Roth reached my side, running around to herd the refugees.

But for every one we managed to protect and hurry toward the portal, more ran in other directions. I wanted to yell, but my head was pounding, and I felt the drain from Nuri being on the other side of the portal. It also transmitted across my bonds with my other mythicals, and Roth and Zephyr were struggling.

Sen leaped up Zephyr and onto his shoulder and simply hung on, the myconid having nothing left.

As I came close to a mother and a terrified daughter struggling to make progress, I swept the girl into my arms, grabbed the mother, and ran toward the portal. The soldiers around me did the same as Seth, his fire fox, Zephyr, and the major covered our retreat.

There was nothing I could do anymore to save everyone, but I was going to save those I could. With any luck, we'd get reinforcements before they overran us.

Thankfully the dark elves from the patrol hung back, worn out. They had been hit fairly hard in our first attack. The second group with tracking animals was concentrating on chasing refugees. I saw Aolis shoot a dark elf with the gun we'd given him, but I didn't see if he had hit his target.

An earth elf grabbed the ground near my feet and tripped me by shaking it. I used the air to cushion myself and get upright, my arms still wrapped around the crying child.

The mother beside me almost fell, but I caught her too. A moment later, the ground went still, and we ran.

As the portal became visible on the horizon, I realized I had been running for several minutes unhindered. I had concentrated on fleeing and had been so overwhelmed by the growing ache in my body from having Nuri on the other side of the portal that I hadn't noticed the noise dying down.

The child in my arms quieted as I slowed and glanced around. Twenty or so of the elves we'd rescued were still with us. Some of the sickest and most injured were on Roth's back and the soldiers were carrying children, but the healthier elves who could manage the run had kept their heads and swept their offspring with them.

I didn't see Cherisse or Minsheng, and fear gripped my heart. My Shishou was still out there.

Nuri on Earth, the firebird said, a strange quality infusing the communication. I was surprised it worked over the portal before I remembered the elves I had spoken to and how I had heard them in my head as well.

Is help coming? I asked, frustrated that it had taken so long for him to get there and knowing that meant it would be a considerable length of time before anyone came back through if they did agree to aid us.

We reached the portal unhindered, however, and I quickly ushered the soldiers and refugees through. I stayed on this side despite the pain. I wanted to go and get the rest of the refugees, but I could see the exhaustion on the faces of the elves and the major.

A few ran toward us and we ushered them to safety, but no more appeared. Nuri entered the portal again, drawing my attention back to where I was, and became aware of how little power I had left. Zephyr slipped an arm around me.

"We did what we could," he said. "We rescued those who were able to move with us."

"They've got Minsheng and Cherisse," Seth replied, his fire fox on his shoulders, both of them panting.

"For sure?" I asked as my stomach knotted despite my bonded mythical coming back to me.

Seth nodded, unable to talk.

That was the encouragement I needed. Despite my state, I tried to walk away from Zephyr and head back to find them, but he wouldn't let go of me.

You haven't got the strength. None of us have. It's no good for anyone if we get caught as well because we can't fight. We have a better idea of what we're up against and what we can do. All we have to do is gather our strength and come back.

How will we find them if we don't go after them now?

Zephyr paused. It was a good point, and he knew it. The patrols and the other dark elves hadn't come this far, and we had no way of knowing what they would do with the refugees they had taken.

Okay, we should carefully go back and see if we can get an idea of where they're going. Nothing else. We'll have to act as scouts.

I told everyone to stay by the portal and let whoever came through with Nuri know to wait for further instructions. It wasn't ideal, but nothing that had happened on this planet had been. There were too many unknowns, and everything had been far harder than expected.

We made our way back to the road and the last place we'd seen the refugees, all my mythicals but Nuri with me. Everything was still quiet, and the pain in my stomach lessened when Nuri returned through the portal.

Although it had been difficult on the bond and how connected I felt to the firebird, it hadn't drained my energy as much as I'd feared. That had been handy after battling the dark elves. I dreaded to think how much worse it would have been if I had run out of energy or collapsed partway through.

I might not have been able to stop the dark elves, but I had deterred them from chasing us and saved some of the refugees. It wasn't perfect, but it was better than nothing.

Despite that positivity, all I thought about was my missing friends and what might be happening to them. I didn't know what I'd do if I lost Minsheng. He was one of my constants since the beginning of my crazy life as an elf and then as the Henera. I needed him and his wisdom and understanding.

Cherisse had come here to make a difference. She might have had questionable moments and been difficult about anything she disagreed with me on. Still, she'd been there when it mattered and risked her life alongside mine to rescue these elves and others. I knew which side I wanted her on and how much we'd lose if we lost her.

As we continued, I saw footprints of the refugees who had run in other directions. I could also see a dust cloud off to the left of the road, which implied that people were moving that way.

Can you reach out that far and feel the air and what's moving in it? Zephyr asked when we walked that way. The cloud of kicked-up sand and dirt continued to obscure our view.

I didn't reply, choosing to focus on what he'd suggested. I was worn out as well, and we were out of food and water. As we walked after the group, I scanned the air with my mind for anything moving through it. I wasn't sure I could reach them, but I would try.

As we slowly got closer, thankfully moving faster, my mind touched an air elf who was in control of something. I didn't think I was up to the challenge of fighting him, so I retreated to find another way around.

If the air elf noticed my probing mind, he didn't

respond. He simply continued to move his control along with the group ahead.

I frowned and told Zephyr.

They don't appear to be taking them onto the road. There must be something else out here, he replied.

It wasn't a bad point, and it would explain how they had appeared so quickly during the battle. If the dark elves had a station nearby, there was a good explanation for how they'd caught us since it shouldn't have gone wrong as horribly as it had, not so swiftly.

I focused on the task at hand. I had to locate the place to which these dark elves were going, assuming Zephyr was right.

No sooner had I thought this than Sen bounded off Zephyr's shoulder and scampered ahead. I could feel her fatigue, but she wanted to help, and she was the only one who could get close enough to see what was going on without being detected.

Zephyr slipped an arm around my waist again to help me walk while I focused on what the myconid saw.

She bounded off so fast I felt seasick, but I got used to it. A group the dark elves had captured kicked up a dust cloud. They had the strange tracking creatures with them and surrounded the majority of the refugees we'd tried to rescue.

I noticed that many of them struggled to walk, so they wouldn't have been difficult to catch up with. There were more dark elves than we could take on, even if I had been at full capacity. Several of them were wearing the strange armor we'd seen recently. Some were also wearing weapon-like add-ons.

Sen didn't watch for long before I noticed a sandstone building ahead of them. I thought it would have taken an earth elf a lot of time to harden the sand in the desert and sculpt it.

It was beautiful and yet another example of what the elves were capable of, but it also seemed oppressive. There was a prison-like feel to it. Guards roamed the walls, but they weren't watching for danger from the outside. They were looking in.

Although there was no way to be sure, I guessed the building held elves or mythicals, so we were going to attack it.

Are you seeing this as well? I asked Zephyr.

Glimpses. Someone has to keep us walking in the right direction.

We need to do something.

And we will, once we have more information and rested, and can come back with more of our allies.

Although Zephyr was right that we ought to go back, a huge part of me yearned to do the opposite. I wanted to find out who they were holding in the building and determine if we could do anything to help them.

Sen didn't dare get any closer, however. Her little body was hidden behind one of the last close bushes. If she went any farther, she ran the risk of being seen, and I didn't want her to go into that much danger.

Instead of moving forward, I waited to be sure they were taking our friends and the captured mythicals and elves into the building. Then we went back the way we'd come, calling to Sen to come back to me at the same time.

With a heavy heart, we made our way back to the portal

and toward the friends who were waiting. I could follow the tug on my stomach to Nuri, the firebird having come back before we returned.

I glanced in the direction of the building one last time. As soon as I had rested, we were going back.

CHAPTER SIXTEEN

Standing during the video call with the President and the general, I tried not to get impatient with the questions about what had happened on the elves' home planet. I'd done my best to give them the information they sought, but it felt like they wanted more, and I didn't have time for it.

Although there was nothing stopping me from heading through the portal and getting the people I cared about back, it would go better if I had some of the might more elves and a squad of US soldiers could provide. Simon was summoning elves from the Amcika crew, and Ronan was speaking to those in the Sanctuary.

They had all lost elves who meant something to them. Finding the prison had convinced the groups they needed to give us the best of the best to rescue our people and the refugees.

As always, the humans of this world were less than eager to interfere or risk their lives.

"I understand your fears," I said as I stepped forward

and brought their attention back to me. "And I'll understand if you want to pull out. But the dark elf is coming. He's a threat, whichever way you look at this. They know we've been over there. They have two of our people. I don't know about you, but I want every advantage I can get when that elf comes this way."

"We understand your concern about your friends and this enemy, but our soldiers haven't trained for this, and they're getting hurt in this fight. I have to consider their safety."

"None of them will be safe. None of *you* will be safe if that elf comes through the portal. I don't want anyone to die either. I've lost people who matter to me. I know how much it hurts. But many more will die if we don't take all our opportunities to gain an advantage."

The general frowned, not appreciating my tone or the frustration I didn't try to hide, but the President nodded.

"You make a good point. We'll send more soldiers to aid you. But Aella, I want your word that you'll protect them as you would the mythicals. I'll give them extra weapons for your forces and vehicles if you can get them through the portal. Let's save your legs for fighting."

I exhaled in relief. It was a huge concession for the President to make, and it was likely to save us. I saw the gratitude on Simon's face as I looked around. The Amcika elf had chosen to leave me to make the call with the major alone, and I wasn't going to add another wildcard to the mix. Simon was the reason I'd lost someone, and although he was on my side and had promised no more needless deaths, I still wasn't happy with him.

There had been progress with his research, however. I'd

helped him with some of it, and he was itching to show me what he'd been working on while I'd been through the portal.

The soldiers and elves we'd left behind had excavated more of the immense underground building, clearing the front of it and other rooms, making them solid and livable again. Simon had set up a lab inside one of them.

Although I wanted to rest and then go back to the portal to rescue my friends, I followed him to the lab, and Zephyr came with me. Our other three bonded mythicals were resting, having extended themselves physically and in other ways. Nuri had been exhausted from stretching our bond through the portal. The others had been integral to our plan.

Simon ushered me into the lab. Chris was there as well, studying one of the gauntlets we'd managed to grab from a patrol guard and bring back with us. We'd lost the armor with Aolis, but I was determined to get it and him back. Simon led me to a small device.

"I think I've managed to create some tech, with some help, that we can use to stop the elements from being controlled in specific areas," he said as he switched the device on.

I looked at the front of it. It had four switches on it, each one marked with an element.

"Try it," he said.

Flicking the air switch, I felt a stabbing pain in my head, and my grip on the air barrier I normally held around me released. I gasped as the pain faded and then reached out to the air around me, but my ability was gone. No matter what I did, I couldn't connect to it.

With wide eyes, I flicked the other switches. I wasn't holding on to anything as I pressed the buttons this time and didn't feel any pain, but I was cut off from the elements.

Keep it on, Zephyr said as he walked to the other side of the room.

"Its range is only a couple of yards," Simon said. "Less for a very powerful elf, more for those who are weaker. It's the best we could do with the tech we had, but in theory, it could be made much larger."

"Be careful with this," I said as I flicked air back on and my control returned. "If it got into the wrong human's hands..."

My voice trailed off when I saw the look on Simon's face. He'd considered what it might do as well.

"I understand, but we have to combat the dark elf. And it doesn't work without dwarven components and gnomish tinkering. The humans couldn't make this without our help."

"Good. Let's keep it that way."

Simon nodded but refused to take the device when I tried to give it back to him.

"I'm working on making another. Take that with you. I'll have a better version the next time you come through the portal."

"And I should have a replica of this for you two and Seth," Chris said, not looking up from the bench and the fire gauntlet he was studying.

There was nothing to do but rest until the cavalry arrived, but I went to my tent via the portal. It shimmered in the dim room, making me think of moonlight reflecting off a lake.

It was beautiful but deadly. Elves and soldiers were positioned around the room to guard it, standing in fortified areas the earth elves had constructed for that purpose.

Relieved that we had a line of defense, I went to rest. I tried not to disturb Sen, Roth, and Nuri, who all had their heads down. I grabbed the helmet, though, and held it out for Zephyr to touch. Before we slept, we funneled our leftover power into its crystals.

I'd drained the air crystal while fighting, so we put our leftover power into it, stopping before we drained ourselves. I would not drain myself so much that I broke my bond with my mythicals, but I came as close as I dared.

It felt as if it were barely ten minutes later when Emily appeared at my side, shaking me gently to wake me. The first things I noticed were the pain in my head and the dryness in my mouth. I had not taken care of myself the previous day.

Let's get breakfast, Zephyr said. Sen, Roth, and Nuri were awake as well. I had been the only one still asleep.

Giving Emily a nod, grateful to see a powerful ally, I got up.

"Everyone is here and ready to go when you are," she said as Simon came in with a massive tray of food. I took it and dug in.

"Tell me who I've got," I demanded through my first mouthful of toast.

"The Sanctuary sent a lot more centaurs and healers. Sierrathen and Vestan came as well."

"Both of them?" I asked, almost dropping the sausage I'd picked up.

"Both of them. They said it was time to become more involved in everything. The soldiers arrived with a huge medical team and supplies, whatever the healer elves said they needed. The Amcika elves have their healers and a bunch of earth and water elves. Said they'd keep us supplied with water."

I nodded, grateful for the common sense of everyone. It was the perfect team.

"And we made you more cloaks," Simon added. "Not enough for everyone. Daisy and a few others stitched as fast as they could, but we ran out of fabric. All the centaurs have one, and many healers, medics, and the elves we thought you'd want to bust into a building with have them."

As Zephyr ate beside me, I took in the info. Until I saw everyone, I wasn't sure I would know who I wanted, but I felt better about my options. We could do this.

We ate quickly and I drank plenty of water, knowing I needed to hydrate and get ready to go back through the portal. It wasn't ideal that we'd left the majority of the refugees in the hands of the dark elves, along with everyone else we'd lost in the final battle.

As soon as the team had filled me in on what was new, I asked about the refugees we'd managed to rescue. Many of them were young children.

"They're safe and resting at the Sanctuary," Emily replied.

I sighed in relief. It was the best place for elves who weren't sure of their powers and needed love, care, and time to adjust to this world. They were surrounded by their people, safe and cared for and given time to develop into the people they could become.

"Let me know how they fare?" I asked, knowing Emily had been spending a lot of time there lately.

"Always."

I grinned, then finished eating and drinking and got to my feet. We had work to do, and there was no time to waste. My mythicals got to their feet too. Nuri and Sen came over to sit on a shoulder each. I stroked Roth as I slipped my other hand into Zephyr's. This was my family, and our Shishou needed rescuing.

"Okay," I said. "Let's get a look at my team and what we're taking with us."

It felt weird to say "my team," but no one flinched at the suggestion, so we walked to the entrance. I noticed they had widened it overnight and made the floor smoother. It now sloped down toward the portal room. It was also better lit, with mirrors bringing in light the same way the Sanctuary did in the caves.

The interior would continue to improve. I reached the portal room, and my jaw dropped. The room was almost full, including two desert buggies sitting in front of the portal, looking as if they were going to fit through. On one side of them were twenty soldiers with the major in front of them and another ten medics carrying supplies.

To the other side were elves I'd come to recognize. They were powerful in their own right. Emily went over to join them and left me to stand with my mythicals. She fell in beside Sierrathen and Vestan, the council pair holding hands under their camo robes.

Simon handed me mine, and I put it on as he helped Roth put his on.

After we'd donned what we needed and I'd picked up a pack of food and supplies that I needed to carry as well, I began, "This is a rescue mission. It's going to take some time and a little risk, but our priority is to get to the prison building we saw, breach it stealthily, deal with any threats, and rescue our people and as many others as we can. Any questions?"

There was a resounding silence.

I considered verifying that they knew what they were going to do, but I saw a commander for each group. Ronan stood in front of the centaurs. Sierrathen, Vestan, Seth, and Serfina headed up the elves of each element, and the major was in front of the soldiers. I would give orders to a few people, and my small army would do as I needed them to.

I nodded, grabbed my pack, made sure my helmet was inside, noted that my high-tech bow and arrows were with it, and made my way to the portal.

I hesitated. I could be walking into anything, but my reaction had to be consistent. The sooner I got there, the sooner I could take on whatever lay on the other side and create a window for everyone to follow.

"Give me a couple of minutes to secure the area," I said as I paused in front of the shimmering window. "Then bring the elves, centaurs, and soldiers. Last are the medics and the rest of the equipment."

"Yes, ma'am," and "Yes, Henera," echoed from the portal cavern before I plunged through.

My mythicals came with me. We stayed close as we traveled through the tunnel-like space in between worlds. I could do nothing but wonder and think, the sensations still incredibly strange to me.

We eventually came out the other side, my eyes almost watering in the sun that sat fairly high in the sky and past this planet's midday. I blinked before my eyes adjusted. I pulled an air barrier around us and looked for threats.

Nuri scout, the firebird said from my shoulder. He launched into the air, my barrier unable to protect him as he got higher.

I moved out of the portal with Zephyr and Roth to give the others space to come in behind us and started creating a barrier around the area. It wasn't the perfect way to defend the area, but it was all we had to work with.

I'm coming for you, Minsheng, I thought. *Hold on a little longer.*

CHAPTER SEVENTEEN

When the first elves stepped through the portal, Sierrathen and Vestan still hand in hand, Nuri wheeled to the right and descended again.

What do you see? I asked, my bond stretched far enough that my words were faint.

Elves, he replied, not elaborating.

I frowned, hoping it wasn't a patrol and they wouldn't attack us before we got our entire force through, but Nuri didn't seem panicked and continued to fly toward them.

Sick elves, he added a moment later.

Okay, keep an eye on them and land somewhere near them if you can. Give them hope that I'm returning, but we'll come to them. Is there danger near them?

No. Shelter, but poorly made. Many sick.

I exhaled. It was a good sign that the dark elves had not captured all of them, but it would distract us from our main goal by having a group in the opposite direction to help.

After filling in those who couldn't hear what Nuri had

said, I let them know we had refugees to help and waited for the rest to come through. Thankfully everyone stepped through swiftly, making room for the desert buggies and people still to come.

I continued to hold a barrier as Ronan, the four elementals, the major, and a medic came to my side. Once again, I explained the situation, having the advantage of seeing through Nuri's eyes.

"Let's get them here as quickly as we can and back through the portal," the major said. "If they've been out in this desert overnight and then what appears to be most of the next day on this planet, then they need to get out of the sun and somewhere less dangerous. It leaves us to go infiltrate the building without as many to rescue or worry about."

I didn't disagree. I opted to lead the way, but I left the fire elves and some of the soldiers to guard the portal until we could get back. We needed them the least since we could easily cause devastation to any dark elves who came across us. It was the best of both worlds.

I led the rest forward, following my link with Nuri to make it easy to figure out where I was heading. Sierrathen and Vestan came next. They were looking around with awe, seemingly unbothered by the heat and the glare of the sun.

"I never thought I'd live to get to walk on our home planet," Vestan said a few minutes into our walk.

"I think that goes for all of us," I replied, remembering the look on Cherisse's face when she'd come through. So many had waited for this with no idea if it would happen.

"Maybe one day it will be safe enough that we can come through and explore."

The thought had never occurred to me until I opened my mouth and it came out, but I found myself hoping that it was true. I wanted to believe that we would see better times when this world was safe, but I had no way of knowing it would be for sure.

Thankfully no one responded, the heat silencing most of us as we trudged. The buggies were with us, but there were too many of us to fit in, and they were heavily laden with water and medical supplies. I could see the drivers being careful to navigate over the ground, the occasional rock making the sand deceptively dangerous for such vehicles.

I continued to lead the way for the most part until I was fairly sure I could see the camp ahead. Nestled between two larger dunes and therefore not visible until we were much closer was a group of about thirty refugees.

To my great surprise, Cherisse was with them. I blinked as I saw how they'd survived. She'd worked with an earth elf to make another well, and they'd used spare clothes and vines to make a fabric roof over it all. It was the most makeshift shantytown I'd ever seen, but I was sure it was what had kept them alive.

"You took your time, Henera," she said as I came close enough to talk to. I noticed she was sunburned and tired.

"We thought they'd taken you to a prison or something like it in the other direction. Nuri spotted you when we came back through to head there," I explained as the medics and healing elves with me fanned out and began tending to the wounded and sick.

I noticed that there were quite a few of the most elderly here and that they were also struggling, many in a sleepy stupor, their breathing labored.

"How did you get away from the patrols?"

"It was dark, and there was a lot of commotion. I had an earth elf or two with me, and I got them to lie down. We covered them with sand quickly and then laid our cloaks over the top of our heads."

It was an impressive idea, and I was grateful that she'd kept her head and made it happen. She'd probably saved many of the elves from a fate far worse and in adverse conditions.

"We'll get them safe now. You thought fast and probably saved their lives," I said when Zephyr prompted me to not just think about something so important but say it.

"I was worried for a while there that I had doomed them in another way. Many are too sick to move, and I can't get any more water out of the well. Not yet."

"Eat and rest while we get them out of here and back to the portal," I said as I handed her one of the first snacks I could get out of my bag.

I needn't have bothered as Rick brought up an entire pack and handed it to her. She grinned as she thanked him and dug in, sitting under one edge of the shade.

The soldiers were getting those who had been tended to into a buggy or settled astride a centaur. A couple remained laid out, transferred to stretchers the soldiers could carry and having makeshift shades strung out over them. It was efficient.

I wanted to help heal those who needed it, but it was more important to protect these busy mythicals and humans. I concentrated on keeping an air barrier around it all, cooling the temperature inside, and sending Nuri back into the sky to make sure no patrols spotted us.

Everyone was ready to head out. The shantytown became nothing but the new well surprisingly swiftly and my job almost complete.

I led the way back, our tracks in the sand still able to be followed and my box of colder air around us coming with me. We moved slower on the way back, but I could see some more life in everyone we were rescuing. A few of the elves who had appeared to be unconscious woke up along the way, and the relief and gratitude they displayed when they found out we were carrying them to safety made me tear up.

No part of me doubted how they must have felt overnight and through this morning. It would have been difficult to hold on to any hope. Especially as the sun beat down on them and they ran out of water and the ability to get any more. But the worst of their ordeal was over, and with any luck, they would be safe once more.

When we came close enough to the portal for our teams to spot us, they rushed to help and get the most injured to and through the portal.

Cherisse opted to go through with them and get them situated.

"I want to come back and help rescue the rest," she said to me. "Will you wait for us?"

"I'm going to need to," I replied, noting how many soldiers, medics, and centaurs were going to have to leave with her and the others.

"Keep the place safe," she said with a grin before helping an old man through.

I watched them go, my barrier protecting the area shrinking as the number of people on this side grew smaller. I wasn't planning on wasting my energy when it could be a long afternoon.

The last few were still heading through when Zephyr reached for the vine blade he had in human and dragon form and gave it a shake. A long vine flew out across the ground, forming a line in front of the portal. Along it, flowers bloomed, each one growing fast and spilling seeds.

Zephyr grew more vines from it, twisting them into strong pillars and a roof frame until a strong lattice was just above head height. Large leaves sprouted, providing shade of their own, the plants lush.

"They won't last a very long time in this heat without a constant water source, but it's some shade for now," my dragon said as the entire group automatically moved to shelter underneath.

It wasn't long before Emily reached down, trying to find a water source to feed the plants, but I gently reached out a hand and touched her shoulder.

"If we were going to be here a long time, I would let you, but it's not worth the energy right now. Maybe if this place ends up being somewhere we come through often, and we hold it on this side, but save your power to help more refugees."

Emily looked disappointed, but she nodded and stopped. I got the impression that she wanted to see if she was as powerful as Cherisse, the cult leader sharing the element and being someone to aspire to in some ways.

I couldn't blame my friend, but I also knew we had to think of something bigger than our egos. I'd learned that one the hard way, and I didn't want Emily to have to as well.

Thankfully it was less than an hour before Cherisse and the soldiers and centaurs who had gone back to Earth with the refugees returned. I noticed they had more supplies, food, and water with them as well as elves who were strong adding to our numbers.

I wouldn't say no to having a few more elementals on our side, especially one as good as Cherisse. She made most other water elves look like amateurs. Water was going to be something we'd need before we finished this mission. Of that, I was sure.

While we'd been helping the elves, trudging back and forth and then waiting for our party to return, I had watched the sun drop in the sky, our shadows growing longer and the night closing in.

Not sure I wanted to repeat the incident of the day before and how the dark elves had snuck up on us while we had been walking toward a setting sun, I hesitated. Did I want to take that chance?

They're too far to our right if we go directly, Zephyr pointed out. *I know that you need to be able to keep us safe, but we should get moving. The plants are beginning to wilt, and it's going to take long enough to get there that the sun will be low by the time we're close.*

My dragon was right. I picked up my pack yet again. Despite eating and drinking to keep my strength up, the bag was still heavier than I'd have liked, and I was tired. This was my third day in a row of trekking through the desert, and I didn't appreciate the sand and difficult terrain. Nor the heat.

Still, we were soon trudging onward, this time Sen and Nuri scouting, the target somewhere ahead and not as easily spotted yet. At first, our group mainly moved in silence. None of us wanted to waste our energy or do anything but think of how good it would be to see our friends again.

And my Shishou.

I hadn't realized how much I relied on being able to tell him everything and have him support me and the decisions I'd made. I got the feeling that he wouldn't have agreed with them, but I also got the impression that even if he didn't agree, he was going to let me do it my way and be there for the fallout.

Although I sometimes wished someone would stop me from making an asshat of myself, I appreciated knowing he'd got my back when I did. He was pretty badass.

He'd started teaching me martial arts, and I sometimes forgot how good he was at them. This was no simple part Chinese, part American dwarf. This was someone complicated and technically good at a lot of different things.

I couldn't help but feel guilty for the trouble I'd led him into, especially when we got our first glimpse at the prison ahead again. It was a smudge on the horizon when the sun was setting, and we paused, not wanting to be detected. They would have a better view of us from this angle.

"What's the plan?" Ronan asked as he pulled out his bow, his quiver of arrows slung on his back and his supplies over the sides of his body like saddle bags.

"Those without cloaks are going to need to pause here.

The rest of us who can move slowly and with little to betray our presence will scout closer with me," I said, deciding then and there that I couldn't wait to have an idea of what we were up against. We needed to know before it got dark, and that meant we couldn't wait.

There were over twenty who fell in beside me, despite the stringent rules I'd made. I grinned, grateful for the backup and the skill that had led to the cloaks in the first place. They were saving us in more ways than one, and I wanted to make sure we all had them in the future.

I remembered how we'd hidden from the soldiers on Earth and wondered what had changed. I wasn't going to argue with their usefulness, however.

As a group, we crept closer. I kept the air barrier around us, more to dampen any sound and ensure nobody could overhear us. Zephyr kept any that rippled across the ground from heading forward.

Although there would be elves ahead, and we would eventually butt up against their control, I kept going as we were. The building loomed closer. We wrapped ourselves in our cloaks and moved cautiously from bush to bush.

Nuri continued to fly overhead, and Sen bounded closer as well, the small myconid feeling braver after our second encounter with the area.

While the sun continued to sink, we drew close enough that I could make out what was ahead of us. It was a prison. Dark elves were patrolling high sand walls.

Now we needed to get a glimpse inside at what they were guarding and where.

CHAPTER EIGHTEEN

With my eyes closed and my cloak wrapped around me, I was invisible in the cooling desert. Our shadows were growing longer as Sen finally found a way past the guards on the walls. She snuck behind them and toward a door that was ajar. Before she went through the opening, she glanced off the parapet and into a courtyard.

I gasped as her vision showed me more mythical animals than I had ever seen in one place before. They were caged or kept in shallow pools, and as I took in more of the scene, my heart broke. Here was something worse than death. Animals that should have been running free were being kept in captivity far worse than any zoo.

"We have to get every single living mythical out of that building," I said aloud, wishing I could show the elves and centaurs I was with what was ahead of us. It gained me some looks from the nearby elves, but they didn't know what I was trying to do, and very few of them cared.

No part of me doubted how they would react, however.

Cherisse, Sierrathen, Vestan, and Ronan would do everything needed to rescue the prisoners.

Despite wanting to launch an attack then and there, I reconnected with Sen's vision as she slipped through the nearest doorway and into a tower that led down to the ground floor. It was dark and twisting. A small flame lit the stairs that went around the outside of the tower. There was a large drop in the center of the square structure.

I had to close my eyes since Sen bounded down so fast I felt sick. She stopped at the bottom and ducked into a shadow to see what might lie beyond.

There was another door on both sides of the tower. One was open and led into a corridor inside the wall. The other led out into the courtyard full of mythicals. Although I wanted to see how many mythicals there were and what shape they were in, we also needed to know how many dark elf guards were there and where they'd taken our friends and the refugees.

Sen stayed on target and moved to the corridor. They hadn't lit it any better. I was sure that as soon as night fell, we would have a chance to take this place and sneak through it.

As Sen continued, she came to a larger section of the building, finding a dining area, some kitchens, and finally, prison cells. She bounded up to Minsheng as soon as she saw him, flinging herself at him to hug him. He had been dozing, looking worse for wear and sporting some fresh cuts and bruises.

"It's good to see you, Sen," Minsheng whispered. "Does this mean Aella is close by?"

Sen nodded and hugged his arm before bounding off

him and down the row of prisoners. I spotted elves of ours and many of the other refugees. Some of them were in a bad state, and there were a few children who were upset, but they brightened when they spotted the myconid and realized what that meant.

I worried that they would be too noisy as they grew more hopeful and talkative and draw the attention of some guards, but Minsheng quickly quieted them, working with Serfina to get everyone to stop reacting.

I tried not to worry about them as Sen bounded out of the prison area toward the far door. A dark elf guarded each end of the block, but they looked bored and uninterested. I suspected one of them was asleep. It would be funny if I hadn't seen the conditions everyone lived in.

Sen continued, finding a barracks on the other side of the building in the same place as the prison. Instead of this one having large cells, it had one single large room. It was packed full of bunk beds, and about a third of them sported dark elves.

As I encouraged Sen to hurry through the middle of the room, keeping low, I counted the beds and how many were filling them, reaching forty-eight beds with fourteen dark elves fast asleep. Given we had seen seven other elves around the building, I was pretty sure it meant the place wasn't full.

There was no way to be sure, however, and Sen made her way to a set of stairs that wound into the corner of the next room. It was brighter in there and she hesitated, staying in a shadow near the bottom for a few seconds to look up and listen.

This was possibly the riskiest section that she had to do

yet, but after not hearing anything, she quickly flipped her way up the stairs, pausing a couple from the top to peer up and check that no one was guarding the exit. She stopped on the top step again, pulling her mushroom-top head over the edge enough to view the next floor.

A smaller but more ornate room sat above, several dark elves in there lounging around and eating. It appeared as if they were off-duty and I was sure that they would spot Sen, but despite one mostly looking her way, Sen managed to bound up and into the room and then scurried under the edge of the nearest bit of furniture.

Watching, we waited for another opportunity where she could keep on. Thankfully, the elves were rarely static for long, it seemed, and several got up and made their way somewhere else once they had finished eating.

I could hear them talking in a version of Elvish that was strange enough I wasn't sure what they were saying to each other. Sen didn't get close enough to make it easier; she made a dash for the next piece of furniture and the next until she was across the room. She found the next door shut.

Frowning, I considered what Sen should do next. I could feel her desire to pull the handle and get on with the next part of the task, but it would go badly for us if they discovered her. If they so much as suspected an attack was imminent, they would make this harder on us. As it was, I was worried that there were far too many dark elves for our group to face.

We had plenty of elves compared to normal, but I didn't doubt that this would be a hard fight. It was their territory, and they were better-rested. When Sen reached the edge of the room, she swept the view again, giving me an overview of what was there. They looked calm and strong, but none of them had armor on.

Sen didn't stop when the door opened and a pair of dark elves came through. They were wearing armor, their chest pieces sporting crystals like the commanders of the dark elf patrols had. I wanted to keep an eye on them, but we had no way to know if Sen would get another opportunity to go through the door.

On the other side was a long corridor that split the building in two. More guards stood on either side of a set of double doors. For a second, I was sure they would see Sen, but the two guards were staring at spots on the opposite wall, their backs ramrod straight.

Sen snuck to the other side of the wall, keeping a low profile to make herself harder to see. As she moved closer to the guards, it got harder for them to see her unless they looked down. Growing bolder, she hurried along the wall.

As she got closer to the guard, she stuck her back against the wall and slid along it. There wasn't much in the way of a gap between their feet and the wall. Sen had to slow to a crawl to get past without brushing up against the back of his heels. Eventually, she was on the other side, and I sighed with relief.

Once again, she had nowhere to go, however. They had kept the double doors shut, and the two guards didn't look as if they planned to move to let anyone open up the room. Admittedly, I was pretty sure it wasn't the end of the world if we didn't see what was beyond. How they were guarding it and how we found our way to it made me fairly confident that this was the command center or leader.

And that meant it was where I was going to head. If I cut the head off this garrison's command, it would make it far easier to take everyone out of it and make sure they were free.

Zephyr was growing restless beside me. Everyone in the desert had been waiting a significant amount of time. I might be able to see what was going on and know that this waiting was worth it, but they didn't have a clue that I was exploring an idea.

I had to leave Sen to it and focus on getting our team ready to sneak in and take out dark elves, so I drew what I had gotten from the dryad on the ground. I made a large detailed map of the building and extrapolated a few areas based on the symmetry of the building so far.

It wasn't ideal, but everyone else gathered around, huddling under their cloaks so nobody would see us while we talked about a plan. No sooner had I told them about the courtyard full of captured mythical creatures than they agreed that we had to empty the building.

"I think we should level the building once we finish. If the earth elves have the strength," Zephyr said.

"It's not going to stop them for long. They'll just have to bring in earth elves to rebuild it," I replied.

"They might. But they'll have to decide if it's a good idea, and they'll have to expend more energy than it will cost us to tear it down. And if nothing else, it will make me feel better."

I grinned at the logic; it was like Zephyr to think so. I couldn't argue with him since I agreed.

We needed to get this done, however, and there were still some details to decide on. The most important one was how were we going to get the majority of the prisoners out? We couldn't afford to attack outright and risk our lives and the lives of the refugees, but if it took too long and we got stuck inside the building, we could find ourselves trapped with them.

It was clear we needed to have two teams, one to pick off guards and one to get the refugees to safety. Our reinforcements would get them away and through the portal.

Nuri offered to fly back again carrying a message, and I didn't hesitate to give him some basic instructions for the soldiers and elves waiting for us. We would form a chain of stations and safety points and pass the refugees and any mythical animals that needed guidance or carrying along the way.

And the rest of us were going to send as many dark elves to meet their maker as we could.

As I thought this, I realized how true the statement felt to me. At some point in the last couple of days, I'd gone from struggling to hurt these dark elves to being comfortable with killing them. Seeing the penned-up mythicals had played a part in that. This was the enemy, and they were doing despicable things.

I think wars bring people to the point of having to kill and become comfortable with doing so to some degree, but it's important we keep our compassion. There will be times when mercy will still be the right course of action, Zephyr said.

Although I seldom heard Zephyr speak so seriously, it needed to be said. I didn't want to lose the part of me that made me better than Kirdash. Sometimes it looked like there was very little difference, but I was determined to hold onto the hope that there was one.

The group split in two, the centaurs and healers going with Zephyr and the earth elves to tunnel into the prison and create a new route out of the garrison, and the rest with me to use stealth and power to take out dark elves. I was ready to begin.

Night still hadn't fallen, but our cloaks would conceal us, and we agreed on a signal that would declare either part of our plans fubar before slipping silently into the darkening desert.

I moved quickly, barely aware of Sierrathen and Vestan on either side of me. Emily and Cherisse were behind me with Roth between them, loaded with water. We were going to sneak in through a small gate on the other side of the building that was difficult to get to.

Our earth elementals were taking a direct route. With any luck, we'd clear the place out and then tear it down. These dark elves had no idea what was about to hit them.

CHAPTER NINETEEN

As we snuck around the final corner, I spotted the gate. It was set back into the building, and Sen had made her way to it on the inside, but we still had to get to the gate. It was clear that a small sand rock path had once led up to it, but time or an earth elf had crumbled it until it was no longer safe to walk.

I reached forward with my mind, knowing that there was a chance I'd meet the mind of a dark elf, but there was nothing far enough out for me to feel confident to rebuild the path slowly. I kept it narrow, pulling up sand from the desert floor and hardening it into rock well enough that it would hold under our feet, then I moved forward.

Although I'd feared that it would take considerable time, I found that there was a more solid foundation there to work with, and it was more repairs than construction. I was the only earth elf, however, so I inched over, getting everyone closer to the door.

There was a small chance that the guards would discover us, and the nearer we were to the door, the less distance the air elves would have to float us to begin a fight or the less distance we would have to cover to get inside to avoid detection.

Time ticked by as Zephyr drew closer, his team somewhere underneath the building. He was moving faster than I was, but he had less distance to go and more help. With any luck, we were going to arrive at about the same time, however.

I pushed on, none of us talking to minimize the chance of being detected in the dark. I stopped a couple of times, and we held still as patrols moved overhead, carrying lit torches that shed a faint glow down the wall.

I was surprised to find that none of them reached out with their minds. They wouldn't have detected us anyway. The cloaks protected our presence from that type of detection as well as other kinds.

As soon as each patrolling guard moved on I continued until I was almost at the door.

Ready, Sen, I said when I still had a foot or two of the path to make and solidify. She would need time to open the door, however. The key was there, but the mechanism looked rusted. She had been hiding nearby, sticking in a shadow under her cloak in case anyone came by as well.

Now and then, someone came down the corridor to do a cursory check, but it was clear that they weren't expecting any trouble. No one in this building appeared to expect any trouble.

I was relieved, but our good fortune couldn't last forever. At some point, they would realize they weren't alone. For now, however, I continued on the last few feet. Sen scampered across the floor and leaped to the key.

She tried to turn it with her little arms, but it wouldn't budge. It had rusted shut as I'd feared. While still packing in the sand and using pressure to make it hard enough to hold our weight, I reached out with my mind and started feeling the metal of the lock and key.

Water and time had fused them. I began trying to work the water out and, at the same time, shifting the metal. It was a strange process, reversing what time had done to rust it. It was possible because I could control the earth and water elements. It worked.

It took another minute, and I could stand in front of the door by that time. Sen twisted the key as I reached with my hand and pushed gently. Just as the key hadn't moved, neither did the door. Time had stuck it tight.

I sighed as I felt for it with my mind, and Sen dropped to the floor again and backed off into the shadows. Zephyr was beginning to tunnel up and under the prisoners as I reached into the door. The wood had warped, shifting over time and with lack of use, the hinges giving over time as well until it had wedged.

Trying not to let frustration get the better of me, I worked it loose, moving some of the wood and bending it back enough. At the same time, I reached for the hinges and dealt with the rust there, not wanting them to make noise as the door moved open.

Only when I was sure did I attempt any more, using my mind and hand to push the door open a fraction. It finally moved, making noise, but not masses.

Guard coming, Sen said.

I pulled it closed again and pulled my cloak about me to hide. Everyone behind me caught on and reacted similarly.

Watching through Sen's eyes, I saw the pair of dark elf guards come marching down the corridor. They were coming away from the prison end of the building and toward the other.

Neither of them so much as glanced at the door we were about to enter through, but I noticed that the lock and key were shiny, as if they were almost new.

I lifted an eyebrow, surprised by this, but the coast was soon clear, and I didn't want to linger any longer. Zephyr was in the cell with the first group of prisoners, getting them to help the weakest refugees get clear.

Aware that we would need to make sure they weren't disturbed and no more guards went that way, I pushed open the door once more. Although I moved it swiftly this time, I opened it just enough that we'd be able to slip inside.

As soon as I was inside, I took control of the air, adjusting to the very different marked feeling that filled the building. Most of the area around the Mexican portal had felt marked by Kirdash, but here it was someone or several different someones. It gave me more confidence that I was far enough away from the dark elf that I wouldn't meet him anytime soon.

I threw up a barrier behind and in front of our group. I waited until we were inside before shutting the door again. Our small group made our way straight toward the prison and barracks. Although it was in the direction of dark elves, who weren't currently much of a threat, they were close to our allies and friends, and the other guards wouldn't miss them if we neutralized them swiftly.

While we moved, I also dampened any sound we made,

and marveled that Roth could walk so quietly, his hooves not clipping and clopping as they usually would but moving across the hard rock with a glide that only water could usually achieve.

Grinning, I made my way to the door ahead, reaching forward with my mind to detect any elves before they could see us. There were no guards or patrols between us and the barracks, which encouraged me to pick up the pace.

I paused in front of the open door to the barracks, aware that one false move could wake up more dark elves than my group was likely to be able to cope with, and then I looked at the elves behind me. They were ready and willing, but for now, only the air elves were going to act.

Reaching into the room, I found the eight elves farthest from me and took hold of the air around their heads. I could feel Vestan following me, preparing to do the same, his control almost as swift and as focused as mine was. He controlled the air around the heads of the other six, and slowly we shut off the oxygen supply.

A part of me felt guilty for what we were about to do, but there were far worse ways to go than to suffocate in your sleep. We were going to ensure they never woke again, however.

While we acted, Sen bounded to the other end of the corridor and tucked her head around the corner to make sure we weren't interrupted by other guards. Roth, Emily, Sierrathen, and Erlan were ready and waiting for any other threats that came our way, but they were less likely to be able to stop someone raising the alarm.

Although what we were doing might be considered

ambitious, we were two of the strongest air elves in existence, and if anyone could make it work, we could.

Slowly the breathing of each dark elf grew more labored. None of them could get enough oxygen as I sucked it out of the eight boxes I held. It took all my willpower to keep going and not give in and let them breathe, but I held the boxes in place.

I saw Vestan struggling as time went on, sweat appearing on his forehead and his body shaking, but I couldn't easily hold more boxes than I was and keep the two barriers protecting us as well.

It was almost a relief when the first few dark elves stopped breathing, and I could stop holding the air around them. As soon as I was sure I couldn't feel the pull of air in and out of their lungs, I merged my control with Vestan's, helping him finish the job as well.

The job took several more minutes to take out the last few, but mine died before Vestan's, and I suspected the older Sanctuary elf had struggled to pull the air out of the small areas he'd been holding.

When we finally finished, I exhaled, my body shaking. It was one thing to kill another elf in combat, but to kill fourteen while they slept was different. I had to keep reminding myself that they would have killed us if they'd had the chance. Thinking about the mythicals caged in the courtyard removed my inhibitions too.

After Vestan and I took a moment to recover, I gave the others a nod, and we entered the barracks. We fanned out, double-checking the dark elves' pulses to make sure we hadn't left any alive. I'd done what I needed to, but it was good to check.

After that, I went to the far door. It was also ajar and led to the prison on the other side of the building. Zephyr had taken care of the guards in there. Most were out cold or pinned down by the ground and walls.

That left one big obstacle. I made my way to the stairs. Roth, Sierrathen, and Emily were waiting for me. Sen was halfway up, the grinning myconid happy to scout ahead.

The ones most likely to get the dark elves formed into a cohesive fighting force or raise the alarm were probably up there. We needed to take them out next. I paused in front of my team and put the barriers back in place, then followed using Sen's eyes.

The elves in the room above were still lounging around. It was strange to watch our enemies relaxing. It was easy to see them as monsters and judge them, but they had friends, likes and dislikes, and hobbies like we did.

It made me hesitate. We needed to take out these six elves, but our previous tactic wasn't going to work. They would realize they were struggling to breathe since they were awake.

That meant we had to fight them silently, or they would raise the alarm. While I came up with a strategy and informed my elves where the targets were, Sen carefully made her way to the door on the far side again.

I still wasn't sure what to do. Three of the six dark elves were near the door, and there was a good chance at least one of them could run to safety.

Make door stick, Sen suggested. *Then elves can't run.*

I blinked; the idea was simple but perfect. It wouldn't hold an earth elf, but it would delay the others. I could easily undo it when we were ready to proceed.

I closed my eyes to concentrate, then connected to the door. This one was wood as well, and I slowly warped it, pulling water out of the air and surroundings to make it bend and flex.

Once I was sure I had wedged it in place, I put up a barrier in front of it to prevent sound from reaching anyone on the other side. It wouldn't mask everything, but it would muffle shouts and other loud noises.

That done, I opened my eyes and looked at my allies.

"Time to go," I whispered.

As one, we rushed up the stairs and into the room. We were met with stunned silence, and my team attacked.

I blasted two of the dark elves with air, pinning them to their chairs. Vestan did something similar to the other seated one. Sierrathen and Emily used water from a bowl to blast the faces of two others while Roth ran to them. The final dark elf rushed toward the door, but Sen hit him with a dart.

It wasn't enough to down him, but it drew his attention to her and made him yelp.

My control was challenged by someone in the room but I resisted, finding they were far weaker than me.

Sen managed to hit the elf near her with a second dart as he grabbed at her. Instead of catching her, he went over, and there was a clatter when he hit the floor. I winced at the noise but focused on the two elves I had pinned down. Vestan was advancing on his target. I joined my mind with his, and we reached into their lungs and sucked the air out.

It was a violent way to use our abilities and he grimaced, but the elves were disabled, writhing as hands went to throats that couldn't take in air.

Sen jumped onto the back of a chair and shot another dart. Emily also drew a gun. We were only supposed to use them in emergencies. The weapons were noisy enough to draw attention, but I didn't know how to stop her. This wasn't going to plan.

When one of the elves I was suffocating died, I reached for the plant in the room and grew it quickly toward the elf Emily was about to shoot. When she saw me intervene, she lowered the weapon without firing.

I wrapped the dark elf in the plant, covering her mouth as I tied her up and pulled her off the floor.

Despite how careful we were being, there were still thrashing noises. Sen's victim had made a loud enough noise that the guards would have heard.

My fears were confirmed when the door I'd jammed rattled, followed by a muffled shout. They'd discovered us.

CHAPTER TWENTY

Sierrathen looked at the door and then at me. We couldn't get caught. There were too many dark elves left for me to fight, and there were lots of mythicals to free.

Emily was the first to get her head around doing what was needed. She concentrated, set her jaw, and before anyone could intervene, the water elf I'd bound went stiff, her eyes bulging. Blood started leaking out of her ears, eyes, and mouth.

I reached toward the dark elf to figure out what Emily had done. She'd prevented the blood from flowing and was keeping her heart still.

The result was far worse than my attempts to stop the air, since I could see the pain on the dark elf's face. It was effective, however. The dark elf was soon limp, hanging in the plant I'd bound her with.

Although she didn't look happy about it, Sierrathen followed suit. The two elves that Vestan and I were asphyxiating died as well.

We were angry that these dark elves were abusing and

neglecting a compound full of beautiful creatures. I had learned enough to make me livid and our enemies dead.

We turned our attention to the door. Roth clopped over. It had gone quiet on the other side, and I reached out to determine what was happening. I brushed the control of an earth elf who was trying to fix the door. It was impressive since they worked around the water they couldn't remove, though it wouldn't be long before they could open it again.

Moving forward, I located the two guards on the other side. They were standing near this door, the door on the far side and whatever lay beyond it forgotten. I grinned and, following Emily's example, grabbed the blood and the hearts and made them stop.

The attack on the door ended as the elves fell to the floor and writhed. Unable to get oxygen from their blood, they passed out and died. At the same time, I pulled the water back out of the door and unbent it, finishing the job they had started.

It wasn't perfect, but it was good enough that Roth grabbed the handle with his teeth and pulled it open. Vestan went through first, exhaling as he saw the dead elves. He put up another barrier ahead of us to give the rest of the team a chance to get further into the corridor.

I was pretty sure that we'd finally dealt with over half the elves inside the compound, none between us and the prison guards our allies had incapacitated.

We've got the refugees safe as well, Zephyr said as we crept toward the double doors that Sen hadn't bothered to get through.

Give them a moment to get further clear and then start

pushing through to the courtyard and the mythicals, I replied.

So far, this attack had been a success, but it had a cost. I was draining my abilities faster than normal since juggling multiple elements was more exhausting than juggling one.

It also required more effort to insert my control into someone's body and attack them from the inside. It was like the body defended itself against an invading mind on another level. That said, so far, nothing had been able to stop us.

We were standing in front of the double doors. My mind was reaching through when a horn blared from the courtyard to our right, and we heard shouting.

They've seen us, Zephyr said. Some of the mythicals panicked, and one of the elves we'd rescued bonded with a ferret-like creature.

I took a deep breath, not surprised. We would end up finding mythicals for the elves to bond with if we rescued so many, but I was annoyed that it had given away our plans.

There was nothing else to be done about it, however.

After reinforcing Vestan's barrier, I strode forward and shoved the doors open.

Without checking who was in the room, I reached to control it and pushed out any minds I found as I strode forward.

"Surrender, and I will let you live," I told the dark elf sitting at the head of a table. His ornate chair suggested that he was important. He wore the crystal-powered armor we'd seen before. To his right was another dark elven commander.

No one spoke, and the nearby elves who stepped

forward stopped when their leader raised a hand. I felt more than saw my allies fall in behind me. Sen bounded to my shoulder. Nuri flew in and landed on my other shoulder.

The dark elf examined our group, taking in the firebird.

I didn't move or flinch or relent as I felt his mind probing to feel how much of the room I had in my grasp.

Although I kept the emotion to myself, I was surprised to realize he controlled air and earth, his mind reaching through both.

"I won't say it again," I added.

"You threaten me?" he asked as he stood. "I know you think you're powerful, but the dark elf put me in this position. He bred me for war. To make elves like you beg for mercy."

"And I was created to defeat the dark elf," I replied as I reached past the armor, bearing the pain it caused.

I grabbed the leader's heart and stopped it. His eyes bulged, and his jaw dropped. The other dark elves could tell something was wrong, but I held on through the pain of bypassing the shield his armor created.

A moment later, I let go.

"I don't want to kill you," I said as I stepped closer. "But I will. Tell everyone here to stand down, and you can live to fight another day."

He didn't move as he considered my offer.

"The Henera doesn't forgive weakness," he replied.

"Then he can't be the Henera. The Henera is supposed to be merciful and understand that we're as strong as we're trained to be. That we can't fight every force on every day. That's what the Henera is for."

Although the elf encouraged his soldiers to attack, they hesitated. I took control of the leader's heart as Roth, Sen, and Nuri hurled themselves at the other elf wearing armor. Vestan, Sierrathen, and Emily merged with me to attack the others.

"I will spare anyone who backs down," I said as I crushed the commander's heart.

It was a horrible way to kill him, but I was not going to back down. Two of the four weaker elves lowered their heads and stepped back. Roth crushed the armored elf under his hooves as Nuri turned into a fireball and landed on his armor. The flames flash-heated the metal, making the dark elf scream in pain.

It took the fight out of the other two dark elves, and they surrendered as well.

I lifted the body of the leader and floated him toward the open door to a balcony over the courtyard. I walked beside his body until I was outside, the cool night air welcome on my face after the hot, oppressive rooms I'd been passing through.

I could see battles being fought in the light of the torches around the courtyard and knew I needed to get everyone's attention.

Nuri came to me, having read my mind, and flew a loop of the courtyard as a ball of fire before coming back to the balcony. At the same time, I created a large ball of flame in my hand and held it in front of their commander.

"Dark elves of Kirdash. Your commander has fallen by my hand. I am the true Henera. I'll offer you the same mercy I did him. Surrender to me and my allies, and you will live to see another day. You may go where you will and do as you wish, but you will not harm another elf or mythical."

Some of the dark elves hesitated, but others kept fighting. I grabbed the plants nearest them.

After swiftly wrapping them up, I lifted them into the air and lit fires around them, close enough that it wouldn't take much to burn them alive.

None of them struggled once they realized the danger they were in. The rest adopted the same subservient attitudes as the four elves behind me.

"Good. We're freeing every mythical and every prisoner, and we're leaving. The rest of you can make your way to the barracks. We're going to shut you inside for a while. When we've gone, you can make your way out and go anywhere you wish."

Without another word, I caused another vine to grow and hold the commander in place, his dead body hanging over the edge of the balcony, a disgusting reminder that they had lost. Then I used my mind to remove his armor. I would not leave something that valuable behind.

He had a shield on his back as well, which I detached. My allies and Zephyr freed the mythicals below, receiving roars and chirps of delight. I encouraged the elves with me to get down there and help. It was time to get out of here.

The remaining dark elves didn't put up a fight despite their superior numbers. Zephyr donned the armor I'd taken off the commander. Vestan took the set from the lieutenant, and Cherisse was wearing armor when she joined us, escorting its previous owner.

The dark elves took in their dead companions and a few dared to show sadness, but most of them were surprisingly indifferent. Although they didn't want to die, they apparently didn't care for each other.

I tried to hide my reaction, but one of them stepped forward.

"Where was your mercy?" he asked.

"I'd have given you mercy if I'd had the chance, but would even one of you have realized you couldn't beat me if I hadn't killed so many and your commander?" I replied.

The dark elf opened his mouth to argue, then nodded.

"The...dark elf teaches us to show no mercy or weakness."

"Mercy isn't weakness. Neither is failing. Weakness is letting fear change you into something less than the best you can be. Weakness is not trying to grow. Weakness is insecure rulers not trusting that their deeds will speak for themselves," I replied, spitting the last phrase.

I wasn't sure they believed me or were listening, but the dark elf who had challenged me didn't look away.

"Would you answer one question, powerful one?"

"If you make it quick."

"What will you do with the mythicals?" he asked, studying my face.

"We will take care of them and give them the opportunity to be free or bond with an elf who will cherish them, as we do with our mythicals."

The dark elf raised his eyebrows, then relaxed. "Then you are truly more than you appear. I would not call you Henera, but you are not my enemy."

"Anyone I do not call an enemy I call a friend," I replied, wondering if that was going too far, but the elf brightened.

"Then perhaps we will meet again in better circumstances." He stepped back to join the others, and I was left to my work.

We shut the dark elves into the barracks, using our ability to block them in. Then we made our way to the prison and the tunnel Zephyr and his allies had formed into the building. Many of the mythicals were leaving through the new exit. Some of the water-based mythicals had to be transported in containers or otherwise protected from the heat.

I was helping Cherisse lift a bucket full of fish when an otter-like creature, sleek and moving so fast it was almost a blur, rushed up. It was still a couple of feet away from Cherisse when there was a flash of light, and it stopped in the middle of its movement.

A grin spread across the cult elf's face as she reached for the wet creature. It leaped into her outstretched arms and nuzzled her. I was stunned that a second bonding had happened, but I was also delighted. It was a good sign that we were supposed to come here.

Understanding we shouldn't linger, Cherisse encouraged the creature onto her shoulder. The cult leader was glowing with delight. I was genuinely pleased for her and found myself smiling. This made what I had done worth it.

After another half-hour, the majority of the mythicals had been escorted, carried, or encouraged down the tunnel to safety. Very few of them needed encouragement since the creatures saw that the mythicals with us were cared for, in good health, and free to operate.

A few were sick, including the most beautiful unicorn I had ever seen. Also, some fire salamanders and a group of birds were too scared and weary to leave.

Nuri went into the aviary to coax them out, but there were a few who couldn't fly.

"Let me help," Vestan said from behind me. "Orthelo taught me to care for injured birds. It's important to keep them from struggling and tuck their bodies into little pouches."

I didn't argue when the elf pulled a many-pouched apron from his bag and put it on.

Vestan used the air he controlled and his hands to pin down each bird and gently tuck them into a pouch of the appropriate size, adjusting as necessary.

As he worked, he explained what he was doing. Zephyr and I joined him, tucking birds into pockets until he carried twenty of them. There was a large, wary bird of prey near the back of the aviary that we turned our attention to last. It had a broken wing, and it had lost a lot of feathers.

No sooner had Vestan opened the door of its cage, far braver in front of the large bird than I was, when there was another flash, and Vestan gasped. A whoop of delight behind me made me whirl. Sierrathen looked delighted.

I had seen both of the Sanctuary elves conduct bonding ceremonies but only now realized what it meant to them to get the opportunity to bond. This was a special moment for a person who had regular reminders of their lack.

I sighed as the bird willingly shuffled to him, and Vestan helped it onto his shoulder.

I had done something special for so many this night. I slipped my hand into Zephyr's. This mission had been a huge success.

CHAPTER TWENTY-ONE

The portal loomed ahead, a pale, shimmering light to guide us in the dark. Although I was still a fair distance away, I could still make out the silhouettes of the rescued refugees and mythicals making their way to Earth. I was lighthearted and happy, knowing I'd played a huge part in getting them to safety.

I was also exhausted.

I was sure we would benefit from everyone we had gained so fast, although I was concerned about the sickest creatures. It would take a lot of work to get them better and back on their feet. If Orthelo could guide us, we could bring the vast majority back to good health and strength. A small part of me wondered if I could use my abilities to help the rest.

Not long ago, I had stood in a tent and focused on merging my control with four other elemental elves as they worked to save Cherisse. If the dark elf could heal and regenerate his body, there was a chance I could repair the ailing creatures. The anatomy of the mythicals differed from what I was used to, but I would learn.

I was thinking about this and how we would get everyone to the Sanctuary to rest and recover when I noticed that people were coming through the portal to this planet. Someone shouted my name.

The voice had enough panic in it that I jogged toward the portal and waved. Simon, Chris, and some bruised soldiers were running toward me.

"What's wrong?"

"Not all of the refugees were as helpless as we realized," Simon said as Chris panted and frowned.

I stopped, not sure I understood.

"They were spies," Chris said. "When we started to load them into the transports, they hit us with powerful abilities and ran for it."

"How many?" I asked.

"At least six. Maybe more."

Shitsticks, I thought, then said. That wasn't what we needed. That was a large enough team that if they were powerful, they could do lots of damage. I would struggle to stop them.

"Did they give any indication of what they hoped to achieve?"

Simon, Chris, and all but one of the soldiers shook their heads. I looked at the one who hadn't responded and gave him my full attention.

"What do you know or suspect?" I asked. I needed something to go on.

"The portals. They mentioned hearing one was open

somewhere, and there was another one the dark elf wanted open."

I exhaled. That wasn't good news.

"It gets worse," the soldier said.

We waited for him to explain.

"I think someone on Earth helped them. A car lurking nearby picked them up, and they knew it was coming."

The words sent a chill down my spine. If someone on Earth had helped them, they had planned this. Someone I had been on missions with had gotten a message to the refugees after earning our trust, and they had managed to do so without me noticing.

I couldn't understand how this had been possible. Surely I'd have noticed? But then, my mythicals and I often carried out tasks and missions alone. We had been focused on protecting people. Had one of my allies had the opportunity?

We can't be sure, Zephyr said. *But there's no point worrying now. We need to get the rest of these mythicals safe, then we can figure it out.*

Although Zephyr was right, I couldn't move. This scenario had never occurred to me. When we'd talked about opening the portal and the risk it presented to everyone on Earth, none of us had spoken of the threat to Earth if we lost control of one. A rogue group of elves hadn't been a consideration.

And it didn't make sense. It shouldn't have been a problem. We hadn't rescued any dark elves.

Come on, Aella. We've got to get these creatures safe. They need us. We'll figure the rest out. We always do. Zephyr pulled me out of the spiral of thoughts I was feeling, and I refocused.

The last of the mythicals were approaching the portal, but some were wary. It was a shame we couldn't bond with them and reassure them, but the elves and soldiers were either coaxing them through or catching them and taking them through anyway. It was a strange sight, but I joined in, using my abilities to help where needed.

By the time the last elf strode through, cuddling one of the sphinxlike creatures I'd first seen in LA two years earlier in the hands of a part-gnome, I was drained, and my head was pounding. There was spare energy in the helmet I wore, and the elves still guarding the portal had crystals and tablets, so we weren't in danger.

Still, it was a relief to usher the last of our allies through the portal and head after them, leaving this inhospitable planet once more.

I tried not to panic during the strange journey to Earth, but it seemed as if it took forever. My thoughts turned to who had betrayed us and what I'd find.

I was devastated that what we'd hoped would be a rescue mission and benefit us had increased the danger to Earth. There was nothing for it but to deal with the repercussions, however.

When I emerged from the portal, Zephyr beside me and my other mythicals in front, there was chaos in the portal room. Mythicals, elves, and soldiers occupied the available space, and they were making a lot of noise.

Coming through the portal had upset the more emotionally fragile mythicals, and people were doing their best to calm them. Sen bounded over to a dryad to help her get to a safe spot. I moved toward the fire salamanders since they were heating up and fire was a real risk.

Newton appeared a moment later, changing to a deep blue and making cute happy noises. It calmed them, and I cooled the area just in case. Then I helped a small bird fly to the door, giving it a way out. Some of them might fly away and not come back, but we couldn't prevent that. At least they'd be free.

A lot of the mythicals seemed lost. Soldiers were imprisoning them again, holding them in containers so we could get them organized.

With any luck, we would be able to take them to the Sanctuary and let them have new homes.

In the chaos, I worked my way to the exit. It was still dark on Earth, and I had no idea what time it was. I was pretty sure the days were shorter on the elves' homeworld, but I wasn't sure by how much.

Outside, I found an array of large vehicles and more soldiers. They were loading refugees and mythicals into the transport vehicles, medics going with the worst of the injured and the elderly. Everyone appeared to be stable, and they were smiling. Many were wrapped in blankets and clutching food and beverages. Some children had toys.

When they saw me, I heard murmurs of "Henera," and people reached out to squeeze my hand and thank me. It added to my emotional chaos, but I smiled back and tried to be grateful for the good we'd done.

When I reached the major, I veered off. There were more than enough people getting the trucks loaded to go to the Sanctuary, and the centaurs and elves who had come from there were going to head back, except for Sierrathen, Seth, and Dyneira.

They came over when we started an impromptu meeting. A moment later, Cherisse was at my side, and Minsheng joined us a few seconds after that. He had the dryad Sen had helped in a potted plant in his hands, the creature's roots deep in the dirt. She looked much happier.

Daisy gave me a nod as she found a plastic box for the fire salamanders and worked with Ethan and Newton to get them to climb inside. Her face was glowing, and it was clear she was in her element, having so many creatures to look after.

Before I could do more than exhale, I heard a thrum. I looked up to see a helicopter coming toward us.

Whoever was flying it had the sense to remain at a distance. Several soldiers rushed that way with bright flashlights to help it find a flat spot to touch down.

"The general," the major explained. "He thought it would be better to discuss this in person. We should go to the main tent to meet him."

"Can we get some food as well?" I asked. I would not be getting any rest before I went after the elves who had run off.

We couldn't let them get away, and it was my fault, so I didn't expect anyone else to hunt them down. Maybe a few would volunteer.

"Already on its way," he replied, grinning. He was used to elves and our need for food when we had spent our energy.

I was grateful and thanked him before my inner turmoil returned. Why had I not seen that some of the elves we'd rescued served Kirdash? How had I not picked up on a mole in our ranks, even if this one served a different enemy.

It wasn't just on your shoulders, Zephyr said.

He was angry too, and I wondered if it was directed at me. Then I realized he was upset with himself. He felt as I did, that he'd let himself down like I thought I had let everyone down.

Before I could reply, we reached the tent, and the general caught up with us. Minsheng put the pot down. Cherisse, Zephyr, and I went straight for the food on a large platter near the command desk.

I grabbed some French fries and bit into one before turning to the rest of the room.

"Okay, someone tell me what the hell happened and why this place is in disarray unbecoming of the US Army," the general demanded.

"My fault," I replied before Cherisse or Zephyr could speak.

Everyone turned to us, eyebrows lifting or otherwise showing surprise.

I looked at Cherisse and Zephyr. They also felt guilty, but I should have foreseen this.

"From what I understand about what happened here, I focused so much on getting these elves here that I never stopped to think if we should," I said. "When I realized they were mistreating captive mythicals as well, I lost sight of our safety and let some enemies slip through."

Zephyr rumbled in discontent, but I didn't give him a chance to speak.

"I will hunt them down and ensure they can't get to the

portals. I think we should look into closing this one as well and guard it or bury it for now."

"No," Cherisse said after I stopped speaking.

She looked at me as she stroked the creature she'd bonded with. Its body was draped around her neck, and its head nestled against her neck under her ear. I opened my mouth to ask what she meant, but she lifted her other hand.

"It was my fault. I was so insistent that we should rescue whoever we found that I forgot to think about our security and what would happen if things went wrong. I've been doing too much of that, and it's gotten me into trouble once already. I shouldn't have made the same mistake twice."

Zephyr stepped forward, his jaw set. "I should have known better. My memories show both kinds of elves working with the dark elf. You two had no idea that they could be a threat or side with him."

"That's enough, all three of you." Minsheng's voice was firm as he stepped forward. "We knew there were risks when we agreed to this mission. You can blame yourselves all you want. All the three of you are guilty of is wanting to give every elf a chance and using your abilities to protect people and mythicals."

I tried to speak, but my Shishou stopped me.

"Yes, there are some risks that aren't worth taking, but you underestimate the good you have done tonight. There are several hundred mythicals out there, five of which have bonded with elves and many more of whom I'm sure will bond with other elves as soon as they're in the Sanctuary. That alone will aid us more than you think. That doesn't include the hundred and something elves who are safe on this planet to recover and grow. They will stand beside us if need be and help defend this planet."

"Hear, hear," the major said. "I met a lot of elves today who promised to help in any battle I faced in the future."

"I know the masters in the Sanctuary can help them find their powers and their health, and we will become an even bigger force to reckon with." Sierrathen stepped forward. "You've given us something we lacked: more of our kind and more mythicals to bond with. There were difficulties in the past, and we took on more dangers than we should have, but the truth is, the dark elf was doing everything he could to get back here. It was just a matter of time, and you have all worked tirelessly to make us stronger."

"Not to mention that the human race is far more prepared than we might have been had you continued to hide in the shadows," the general added.

"None of us blames the three of you for anything." Dyneira bowed.

I exhaled, seeing the trust and belief in every face. We might be in danger, but we were something we'd never been before: united on one team.

CHAPTER TWENTY-TWO

"Okay," I said after I finished eating. Everyone had said everything they needed to for everyone to have the big picture. "It's clear there is a faction of the mythical races on Earth who believe Kirdash will bring them something they think they lack. He must know we have a second portal open."

"Sadly, yes. We should close it if we can," the general said. "I know it's an important connection for you, but it's more a danger than a benefit."

"I agree," I replied.

"The Sanctuary is struggling to find a way to close them," Sierrathen replied.

"The organization as well," Minsheng confessed. "It's as if the great elves of old thought we wouldn't need them again. That they would remain closed until the threat was gone, then no one would ever want them closed again."

It was a logic born of hope and faith that the Henera would save the day, and I didn't doubt it had seemed like the right thing, but part of me wished someone had doubted it and left us the information.

"So, we bury it." I gave Cherisse an apologetic look. Another potential home was about to be lost. She and her elves had been through so much.

It also stretched our earth elves thinner to keep two portals buried and monitor them from afar. It would make it easier for Kirdash to mount an attack. We had to protect two portals. He could attack through one, knowing that if he hit swiftly and hard enough, we wouldn't be able to bring reinforcements to the right portal in time.

Anger at myself rose, but I pushed it away. I didn't have time to wallow in my emotions. I had to make sure we did our best to put this right.

"We should protect all three portals as best we can. It's worth seeing if there are more in other countries. The slave elf I connected with thought there were many, and we should know about more of them. Maybe other governments are hiding the ones they control." I sighed as I finished speaking, imagining how devastating it would be if we'd successfully protected the US to find a large army in Australia or Egypt.

"And the elves that support this dark leader?" the general asked. "I know tracking them won't be easy, and you need to rest, but we have to stop them. We have to defend the portal sites as well."

I nodded. It was a given that they would focus on making us weaker so their allies could come through the portal.

"Ronan's brother and I can help there," Dyneira said.

"We've been tracking mythicals, even in vehicles, for years. If anyone can find where they went, we can."

I didn't argue about someone stepping into that role. The centaurs had repeatedly proved that if they said they could handle something, they could.

"Do as you think best to find them, and I'll deal with them once you do," I replied.

"Not alone, you won't. They betrayed what I stand for as well," Cherisse countered. Her face made it clear that she planned on taking the fight to them as well.

I nodded, not willing to turn down help we were likely to need.

"Get some rest, Henera," Dyneira said. Then she stepped forward and reached for my shoulders. After bending until our foreheads touched, she looked me in the eye. "It's an honor to serve you once more."

Without another word, she hurried out of the tent and shouted for the other centaurs. They would look for the enemy, and they'd contact me the second they found them.

"Rest is a good idea. I'll brief the President, and we'll work on how to bury this portal." The general got to his feet, looking as weary as I felt.

My head continued to throb, my powers not having recovered since I got back. Zephyr and the rest of my mythicals came with me as I made my way to the tent someone had brought up from the Mexican site and set up for me. Mentally thanking whoever was looking after me, I flopped down on the cushioned area. Zephyr joined me.

There was a tub of water for Roth, a saucer of water for Sen, and a perch for Nuri. All three occupied their resting places. As well as draining ourselves, we'd been awake for a long time, and we were exhausted.

Although fear gripped my heart, I was so exhausted that I fell asleep in seconds. At one point, I was aware of Zephyr slipping his arm over my waist, but even that seemed like a background sensation.

I was shaken awake by a rough hand.

"Attack," Minsheng said when I opened my eyes.

Sitting bolt upright, I called to my mythicals in my mind, yelling for them to wake up and help us.

"Where?" I asked.

"Portal. We need to push them back and bury it."

I exhaled and nodded. Then I grabbed my helmet and put it on, along with the metal gloves that helped me direct air blasts.

Armor up, I told Sen as she stirred. Roth stood up. Nuri flew out of the tent as Minsheng hurried away. I grabbed my bow. Although I had not used it much in battle, it was useful and a backup if my powers did run out.

I also slipped a dart gun into one pocket. Zephyr did the same.

Worried this was the beginning of a fight we couldn't handle, I hurried out. A soldier held up some of the bread rolls filled with bacon they were handing out. Zephyr and I raised our hands and he threw a couple to us, then two more.

Not wanting to waste them, I used my air abilities to catch mine and float them over. I took a large bite as I jogged toward the building's entrance and the chaos coming from it.

I heard gunshots and water whooshing and grunts and

shouts as people got hurt. I picked up my pace, eating quickly and reaching forward. This wasn't going to be an easy fight. There were a lot of people packed into a small space, and they were slinging elements around.

Several times the entire area shook and the building rocked. If we hadn't been used to it, it would have been terrifying, but we lifted ourselves off the ground with our air powers and flew toward the battle instead.

I merged with Zephyr and other allies to help them seize the elements in the area so the dark elves pouring through the portal would have nothing to work with.

"We can blow the thing right now if we can get everyone out of there," the major said when he appeared at my side. "Can you hold it and everyone we don't want inside?"

"Probably," Zephyr replied. We stopped at the entrance.

"Good enough." He gave the soldier with him a nod, and the man ran toward the main tent.

"Fall back," I yelled, my voice cracking under the strain.

The major echoed my words as he stepped into the building. I used the air near him to propel his command forward and continued working with Zephyr and the other elves to seize control.

At first, no one responded, but the battle slowly changed direction. Zephyr and I stood side by side, protecting the small force as they retreated.

Mythicals, elves, dwarves, and soldiers poured out, obeying the command despite its illogical nature. The dark elves tried to follow, but I rose into the air and used the gloves I was wearing to direct precise air blasts over my allies' heads to repel our enemies.

At the same time, I started swirling around the air inside with Zephyr's help, creating an indoor whirlwind that made it harder for anyone still in the larger portal room to leave it.

It caught up a few of my allies, but Zephyr soon aided them, giving them a boost and drawing on an air tablet he also carried as the rest ran out and past us, standing behind and helping us form a wall. We then calmly held back the tide as one hive mind, and there weren't enough dark elves to begin challenging us.

More dark elves came through the portal, but they hesitated inside, and Minsheng and the major came running past us. Seth and his fire fox were the last pair with them, a fraction of a second behind.

"All clear," the major told us.

"We'll hold it. Bring it down on the portal, and we'll pack it in as tightly as we can."

"It's full of dark elves," Minsheng pointed out.

"I know," I replied. I sounded callous, but there was nothing else I could do. We could stop them from advancing and hold them inside the building, but I didn't think we could push them back through.

My Shishou either realized this or knew this wasn't the time to discuss it. He backed up to stand beside me as well, raising a gun and waiting to see if he needed to use it.

There were a few more yells from behind me, but I couldn't make out what was said as I blasted dark elf after dark elf back and spun the whirlwind in the portal room faster.

With more coming through the portal every moment,

they tested my control. I held firm, drawing the power I needed from the helmet.

There was a final shout, then an explosion inside the building. I let go of everything, allowing it to react to the detonation. I blasted anything that came out back into the structure. The third loud bang brought the walls down.

It collapsed on the portal, the hillside denting where it caved in. I stepped back, blocking the air blast and dust but reaching for the ground, wondering if the dark elves we had pinned inside were alive or if the explosion had sent some back through the portal.

Although it was a grisly task, I quickly found that there were a lot of dead bodies. Most of the dark elves had been killed by the explosions, but a few still lived, the ones buried in the collapse.

I hesitated. Should I let them die? Should I kill them and put them out of their misery, or should I capture them?

There's a risk to all the options, but I think we need to show mercy at this point, Zephyr offered.

Thankful someone else was leaning in the direction my heart wanted to, we approached the settling rubble and shifted the ground until we'd made a funnel for air to get to the dark elves. We were moving a large chunk of building to one side slowly near one of the dark elves when the weak brush of a mind moved the dirt near us.

The dark elf there was an earth elemental, so I pulled back to let them know we were friendly. All told, we connected with five dark elves who were still alive. Three of them made it obvious, but for the other two, their shallow breathing was all I had to go on.

A medic was on-site, and he hurried over, also thinking it was better to help these elves. More soldiers and another couple of earth elves from the Sanctuary came over to help too.

We'd gone from defending the area to trying to make a good impression on an enemy who hated us and might always do so, but it felt right.

Thanks to everyone's quick work and the proximity of the dark elves to the surface, we soon dug the first one out. He blinked in surprise and sat shocked and silent as we tended his wounds and healed the worst of his injuries.

When we offered him food, his jaw dropped.

"You care?" he asked.

"Yes. We want mythicals to live in harmony on this planet," I said. "You're welcome to do so if you understand that we don't want Kirdash or any elves who can't be kind or get along and contribute to society to come here."

"But Kirdash is the Henera. He brings light and—"

"Does he?" I asked, cutting the elf off. I was irritated that everyone was brainwashed into believing that. "Does he bring anything but strife and difficulty? He enslaves a lot of elves and holds mythicals captive who could bond the elves. He uses you and keeps the much-needed resources of the planet for himself."

The elf opened his mouth to respond again but closed it and thought about what I'd said. We continued to heal him and work on getting his companions out. If nothing else, he'd see us expending our energy to help them.

Soon, the five dark elves were sitting in the sun, being treated and fed.

Having been betrayed once, no one would let these

dark elves go. That risked having them team up to distract us from keeping Kirdash at bay.

The soldiers eventually escorted the dark elves away. I wasn't sure what would happen to them, but I had more pressing issues. Kirdash knew about two portals, and he was still trying to get through the third one in Texas. We had a fight on our hands, and it was time to get back to my part in it.

CHAPTER TWENTY-THREE

Flying on Zephyr's back with Nuri, Roth, and Sen following us, we made our way to the Sanctuary. We were still waiting for Donnacha and Dyneira to find the dark elves and refugees who had vanished from the second US portal site and it was clear that we would have to enlist help from the Sanctuary.

Since we'd secured the second open portal, there had been news from the Mexican portal that earth elves were trying to clear the rubble there. We'd split the earth elves who were willing to join our cause between the two buried portals to fight the forces that were trying to come through.

The fight came down to the earth elves having to push the dark elves back and defend the area around the portal. The other elementals could only rest and prepare for a fight. A few were still working on shutting the portals again, but they didn't need our interference.

There were only so many books on the subject, and I had no expertise on it. I could make the elements do all sorts of things, and I was good at it, but that wasn't helpful without knowing how to close the portal.

That didn't leave a lot for me to do except anticipate the impending attack. The three portals were under pressure, and I could see only one reason for that. The dark elf was hoping to break through one of them.

Of course, he could focus most of his forces on one and distract us at the other two. He could afford to put his forces in different places since he had the advantage. We had to defend all three since any of the portals might have to withstand a large attack.

There was no easy way to get the mythicals and soldiers from one portal to another quickly. None of them had the coordination to make it easier. If the dark elf broke through at one of the portals and it was undermanned, we were screwed. We had no ability to turn the tide easily.

I couldn't let that happen, which meant asking the Sanctuary for more help. The Mexican portal remained the cult's primary focus and was likely to be kept safe, but the other portals were less well-guarded, and they didn't have a mountain to bring down on top of them to stop the dark elves from breaking out.

It was a precarious situation, and I wasn't happy about it. I was hoping our allies would understand that we needed to act.

When we landed next to the Sanctuary border, the area was quiet. A dwarf waved us through since the inhabitants were used to seeing us.

Before I was halfway to the entrance of the cave network where the Sanctuary council met, the council and the four elven masters came to meet me.

In the past, if I'd seen them moving about the Sanctuary to find me, I'd have wondered what trouble I was in or if I was about to be told something awful had happened. This time they were smiling, and I wasn't sure what to make of that. Did they have good news?

I stopped in front of Orthelo.

"I cannot talk long." He beamed at me. "I wanted to join the others in thanking you for all you have done for our kind and the other mythicals. Many brought here by this world's soldiers need our care but will recover to some degree. It makes my heart glad to see so many offered hope."

"When I found out so many mythicals were being held against their will, I had to free them. I didn't do that alone. Many aided me, including your leaders and guards. We all did this, not just my bonded mythicals and me."

Sierrathen and Vestan nodded, and the other council members dipped their heads.

"I don't think you have come here to be thanked, however," Sierrathen said. "You look tired, and I know you can't have rested for long, if at all, to get here so soon after I did."

Her logic was sound. I hadn't taken much time, just long enough to eat and take necessary breaks mid-flight. The dark elf wouldn't rest, and it was only a matter of time before he pushed through the portals.

"I'm concerned about the two portals on US soil," I said, deciding not to beat around the bush.

"You're not alone in that assessment, but we will not force anyone here to do anything they don't choose to.

Many of our mythicals will come to your aid," Vestan said, although he sounded sad.

"I'm aware of that, but if we don't protect those portals and the dark elf overruns one, the Sanctuary will be in as much danger as everyone else. You need to defend yourselves as much as my people and those Cherisse commands, not to mention the refugees and mythicals we promised to protect."

I thought I saw the corner of Sierrathen's mouth twitch up, and several of the teachers nodded. That was something every mythical should consider. The humans couldn't help much, and the dark elf was doing his best to break through.

"I'll do what I can to persuade my students and the people I interact with," Aquilan said. "It is the least any of us can do for the Henera. You are our great hope, but you shouldn't stand alone. I will make sure my students are better prepared for battle than they have been in the past."

This garnered interest from the others, and the other masters nodded.

"We'll do what we can."

Before I could thank them, although my relief showed on my face, Ronan slipped into a trance. Someone was connecting to him.

I reached for the communication stone Dyneira had given me. It was warm to the touch and glowed. I wrapped my hand around it, and my mind went to another place.

I was standing at the edge of a large lake, the water shallow and crystal-clear. When I turned around, Donnacha and Dyneira stood with Ronan in conversation.

At first, I hesitated to join them, not sure if I'd been

invited to this connection or had hijacked it because I'd been close to another recipient. This wasn't a type of magic I was familiar with.

Ronan noticed me a second later, and his glance drew the other two's attention. Dyneira smiled when she saw my mythicals.

I had to leave them behind a lot recently, Zephyr especially having to either carry me or guard me while I talked to someone in a dangerous situation. This was the first time in ages that the bodies we were leaving vulnerable were safe.

I stepped closer as the centaurs bowed. After returning the gesture, I looked at Dyneira, who was one of my favorite mythicals.

"The elves who came through the portal. They're...not what we expected," Dyneira said. "There are more of them, and they're heading for the Texas portal."

"Other elves are joining them at regular intervals. They're gathering their forces." Donnacha sounded more serious than usual and it made me hesitant to respond, not sure of the appropriate reply.

"We should send as many there as we can," Ronan said. "More will volunteer."

I wasn't sure, but Ronan excused himself to do that. I couldn't deny that it would mean more coming from one of the council members.

I wouldn't express that aloud, so I waited with Donnacha and Dyneira, not sure what they could add.

"Some of those elves..." Dyneira's voice trailed off. "They're very...human. We overheard them talking. They think the US is hiding the portals because the government wants to make sure they control them and everyone who goes through them. They're coming to reclaim them as a symbol of some kind."

I frowned. That was another problem I didn't need, having mythicals think we were hiding something. Of course, we *were* hiding something—that there was an incredibly powerful elf on the other side of it, and he wanted to appropriate everything and everyone. Not something Joe Public needed to know.

Of course, if that meant people would attack, then we protect the portal. We needed to warn the general and give him time to prepare. With that in mind, I wrapped up the discussion.

"Follow them. If you can do something to hinder them without risking yourselves, do so, please. Otherwise, keep your distance and monitor their actions."

I wasn't sure Dyneira would agree, but she eventually nodded.

When the connection dropped, almost everyone had left. I hoped they had gone to rally volunteers, but transport to the nearest portal was a problem since the Sanctuary didn't have many vehicles.

Not every elf had a dragon to ride. If I got there quickly, I wouldn't have much in the way of reinforcements. I was strong, but Donnacha and Dyneira had made it sound as if there were close to a hundred elves of different skill levels and origins trying to get to the Texas portal and open it.

I wanted to scream. The dark elf had gotten into the hearts and minds of humanized elves and other mythicals who'd never known anything but the human world. He had bent them to do his will.

He might not want the planet if he knew what it was like, however. Humanity had a way of rebelling.

Sighing, I pushed the thoughts from my head. They made me angry and desperate, but they didn't change what was needed.

There was a battle to fight.

I passed on what they had told me, and the faces around me went from concerned to fearful. Ronan hadn't explained much, apparently.

"Do you know where they are heading?"

"The Texas portal. If they make trouble there, there is a good chance the dark elf has plans for other locations. If I were him, there wouldn't be only one target." I gazed at them as the seriousness our situation sank in.

"We'll encourage everyone to aid you. The centaurs will carry the first wave. Half our most powerful elves to each portal." Ronan came back as he spoke. There were more centaurs with him, each carrying an elf on their back.

It was my turn to be shocked. They knew what was required.

"Go," said Sierrathen. She had the final say in the Sanctuary council. "We will send more aid to where it is needed as time permits. I trust you to direct us.

"Thank you," I replied as Zephyr leaped into the air and spread his wings.

Nuri wasn't far behind, and I powered up alongside Roth, carrying Sen.

I followed the large dragon, catching up to him before landing on his back. He was on the familiar path to the Texas portal, but I couldn't enjoy it this time. I used my abilities to speed us up, focusing on Roth since the water pegasus still struggled to fly long distances.

It is worth checking in with Donnacha and Dyneira again, Zephyr said when we were a third of the way there. *If the attackers pick up extras and do not go straight, it might be more useful to meet them and stop them in their tracks.*

My dragon had a point, but it was dangerous to connect to someone else mentally while on the move. I wouldn't be in my body. There was a chance I would fall off.

I'll slow down and keep you safe. If you fall, I'll catch you.

A wave of affection and protection came from Zephyr. He would keep me safe.

After pulling out the communication stone Dyneira had given me, I hunkered down, positioning myself on Zephyr's back so I could stay there without being aware. Then I concentrated on the stone and the feeling I got when I was pulled into a mental connection.

At first, nothing happened, and I was afraid I was doing it wrong, or something might have happened to the brave centaur. Thankfully, that only lasted a short while. My mind felt the familiar tug as the stone warmed in my hand.

"You are coming to us?" Dyneira asked when our minds met. None of my mythicals were with me, but it wouldn't have been easy for them to resist the pull to join me.

"On our way. Ronan is bringing more elves as well."

Dyneira relaxed and described where she was in relation to the Texas portal. She promised to leave a marker that Zephyr could spot from the sky if they changed direction.

Not wanting to be connected for long, I let her return

to her body. Then I was back in my body, still safe on Zephyr's back.

After tucking away the communication stone, I gave Zephyr the new directions. He veered to the south to make sure we didn't miss it. It was time to hunt down a group of misguided elves and humans.

CHAPTER TWENTY-FOUR

We flew for another two hours before we saw any sign of our quarry. Zephyr spotted Dyneira first, the centaur having left two large arrows in the Texan dirt to redirect us. I was aware of how close to the Texas portal we had come and that Dyneira had mentioned the group we were pursuing had grown.

It wasn't until we saw it that I realized what she meant. The group was two hundred strong now, and many had guns.

I gulped. We'd faced weapons like that but not recently. This wasn't good.

Zephyr caught up as I connected with my helmet and prepared to attack. I wasn't sure what we could do against so many, and I feared for the others, but Roth stayed high in the air, and Sen clung to his back.

Nuri turned into a fireball and zoomed ahead. I wanted to call to him to be careful, but I wasn't sure if he knew what to be wary of. Instead, I sent him memories of the soldiers firing guns at us and Lorcan dying.

When Zephyr added memories of bullets bouncing off his scales but still hurting, I winced. He had been so young and so much smaller when he first had shots fired at him. It wasn't a good way for a young dragon to start his life.

Nuri fine. Bullets won't hurt, the firebird replied.

I exhaled in relief.

They should pass through me as well, Roth added.

That left Sen, who could be hurt by a bullet, as could Zephyr if they hit him in one of his few vulnerable places. It took a weight off, but I would have to be careful, and so would the centaurs on the ground.

I'd expected there to be two centaurs, but when we caught up, a group had spread out off to one side. The centaurs were keeping their distance as they followed.

The dark enemies finally came into view. They were chanting and shouting, clearly in a party mentality. Some were young, and others were so old they could barely keep up with the excited band.

Should we talk to them to try to get them to stand down? I asked my mythicals as I looked for elves we'd brought through the portal. If we started with them, the attack might fizzle out. I hoped it would, anyway.

They were near the middle and carried guns, although they didn't look as if they knew what to do with them.

Breath weapon, Zephyr replied.

I considered arguing with him, hoping we could get through this without a single shot being fired. Before I could think of a good way to phrase my reasons, they noticed us.

The people at the back spotted us first. Someone

glanced up and saw the fireball blazing behind them that meant mythicals were nearby. They saw Zephyr next and started firing.

I solidified a barrier around Zephyr and me, pushing it out when bullets passed through it. None of them got to us.

I wasn't sure how long I could keep it up, but I was angry that this had gone straight to violence. I had done nothing but help people and make the world a better place for humans and elves. They were shooting at us simply because we wanted to keep them safe from another dark force.

I had to focus on staying on Zephyr's back as he wove back and forth to avoid the worst of the barrage. I reached down with my mind and redirected many of the weapons. I also made some people drop them.

Chaos ensued, and Zephyr took that moment to swoop down and exhale. A thick white cloud enveloped the main group, including the portal elves we'd thought were refugees.

There were more shouts as the people at the front of the group spotted the cordoned-off area where the Texan portal was. Many of the frontrunners opened fire once more, but not at us.

When the soldiers at the gate started going down, I wanted to scream. This couldn't be happening. I was responsible for opening the portal, and this attack was taking place because of that. If I hadn't been set on opening another portal, those soldiers would be alive.

Aella, focus, Zephyr yelled.

I threw up an air wall between the soldiers and their

attackers, giving them time to react while I protected them. They shouted as Zephyr flew us into the base, then we touched down. At the same time, someone attacked my control. I fell off Zephyr, landing on the ground with a *whoomph*.

Groaning, I got to my feet. I felt the stings when Zephyr was hit by bullets, and it was more painful than I remembered. I stayed where I was, reaching out to find that someone controlled a lot of the air, earth, water, and fire.

Something powerful is controlling the elements, but it feels strange. Almost...clean, I said.

Clean? Zephyr replied, blocking bullets as nearby soldiers joined us, using the dragon's bulletproof body for cover.

It's not going to leave a marker on the elements when it's finished. I tried pushing it for control again, but it was too strong and precise. I wondered if I was ever going to be able to use elemental magic.

Zephyr exhaled again, covering the area in a paralyzing white mist. I worried that we'd catch our soldiers in it. It stopped the barrage, and I reached to control it. Once more, another mind challenged mine. I couldn't seem to fight it.

Instead, the gas that we were supposed to be using on our enemies swept back over us, forcing me to maintain a bubble of air around my head. The soldiers donned gas masks, but it got through the skin eventually, and there was nothing I could do about it.

I took a couple of deep breaths and refocused, letting go of everything but the air. I needed to go beyond the control of whoever this was and break up the group. I reached for the helmet I wore and called on its energy to help me.

It might not make much difference, but I had to try. It started helping; the mind I was pushing against gave way as I spotted a shape looming out of the gas.

I assumed it was a soldier, and I pulled the vapor away from us. Then I realized it was an elf carrying something I didn't recognize.

He said something I didn't understand before lifting his hand. A white gemstone shone briefly before I felt the punch of a powerful air elf.

He took my control, including the bubble of air I was holding.

Zephyr leaped at him as I stepped back, my mind reeling. At the same time, I inhaled, not thinking. A lungful of Zephyr's paralyzing vapor hit me, and my head got light. Wobbling as my limbs stiffened, I moved to clear air.

It was like moving through treacle, my body not responsive and everything appearing too slow. My body wasn't in control as I sucked in another breath. This one wasn't as white since the air ahead of me was clear, but it still enhanced the effect, and I fell.

Roth caught me, and Zephyr's tail flicked around me from behind. I couldn't move. My body was stiff. The elf who'd shoved me back continued toward the main building.

I was pretty sure the elf was augmenting his abilities, and what he was using was similar to something we had not been able to get working in the mountain right before we had made it collapse. There was nothing I could do to stop him now, however.

Zephyr inhaled in the cloud he'd breathed out. I wondered what he was doing until he exhaled again and gave me a wide window of safe air to stand in.

Not sure what was going on, I moved, but my fingers only twitched, although my eyes moved. I was stuck, only upright if someone held me in that position.

I could hear yelling, and I wondered if this was how the people we'd paralyzed had felt. Had they been able to tell what was going on around them, or was I partially immune?

There was no way to be sure, but I tried asking Zephyr anyway. Then I realized I couldn't feel my bonds with my mythicals properly. They were still there, and I was aware of them, but it was like something had numbed the bond or muted it. I couldn't talk to them.

As more dark elves moved past me and the gas cloud dissipated, I realized we had lost a lot of soldiers. Many I didn't recognize. I could hear gunshots as well, but no one fired at me. Zephyr and his scales deflected enough bullets that our attackers had learned not to bother.

The elves met with no more resistance. Whoever was leading them was so powerful that with me stuck fast, there was no one who could counter him. I grew more frustrated, willing myself to twitch a finger.

At first, I couldn't do it, and I wondered if it had been a coincidence and something else had made it happen, but eventually, I managed it again, then again.

Hope that I might be able to get back into the fight filled me as the emotions of my mythicals flooded into me. I reeled, feeling their panic.

Soon I was moving my whole hand, however, and the

grip of Zephyr's tail around my waist loosened. I slumped toward him, struggling to get my legs to respond. Slowly, I regained the ability to move all of me.

That was awful, I thought, hoping Zephyr could hear me. *Did it feel different for you too?*

Yes. It was as if you were missing. Cut out of everything.

I shuddered as we rushed after the invaders, and I helped Zephyr protect us from the bullets. It sounded like they were firing fewer shots, but I wasn't sure since my body was still behaving strangely.

Although I was sure it had recovered more swiftly due to my elven nature, I suspected I had inhaled a much smaller dose of Zephyr's breath weapon than others. My body was almost back to normal.

While we made our way to the building, I felt for what elements were controlled and by whom. Sometimes I brushed the strange device's control, and sometimes it was another elf. For now, I didn't try to challenge the main elf, working instead on knocking everyone else back.

It gave me some elements to work with, and I blasted a large swathe of elves out of the way. When I reached the entrance to the building, I was relieved to see that a lot of soldiers were still alive. They had retreated inside and were shooting at the elves and humans.

Part of me was devastated at the many dead or wounded, but I couldn't expect the soldiers to fire back with darts when the attackers were using real bullets and trying to kill.

No one had been able to stop the advance of the elves, however, and I could see them in the portal room ahead. Keeping an air barrier around myself and my mythicals, I hurried forward, ignoring the majority of the humans. I had to protect the portal.

Zephyr took human form, and a bullet bounced off his skin a moment later. That never ceased to amaze me, and it reminded me that he was the least vulnerable of us all.

His mind melded with mine and strengthened it as he came closer, extending the air barrier around me and making it thicker. I felt his desire to protect me as more bullets came our way. The attackers had realized that we were heading to the portal room to stop them from opening it.

Roth blasted several with water as I sucked more from a nearby water pipe. Sen darted around, wearing her dragon scale armor and knocking humans out with darts and ice. Nuri flew over everyone's heads, putting people off shots more than setting them on fire as he swooped close to them.

I hit many with air, and Zephyr used the dagger and the vines it could create to grab and hold others. I also noticed him using the plants to crush weapons and lift them out of reach in an attempt to end this fight.

We slowly pushed into the heart of the building. It held more staring mythicals and part-mythicals. I could feel the barrier that Chris had constructed protecting the area from magic used inside. The elf carrying the elemental device stood near it, his face contorted as he wrestled with the pillars.

It was clear many hadn't seen anything like the portal before and hadn't expected it to be real.

I stepped into the protected area and brushed the control of the elf. He glanced at me, his body inside the pillars' forcefield, no doubt wrestling with it. I had been here before, but this was going to be one of the hardest fights of my life.

I couldn't afford to lose.

A third portal could not open.

CHAPTER TWENTY-FIVE

Before I could make my first move, someone fired. The bullet hit the air barrier around me, slowing and coming to a stop inches from my skin. When it did, others began firing.

Terrified, I crouched and made the air barrier thicker. Zephyr strengthened me until I could stand again, pushing outward and sucking the heat out as Simon had done. It slowed the bullets more quickly, and after that, none of them got close.

We'll stop the ones out here. Take out the main elf, Zephyr told me as our eyes met.

I nodded and turned back to my task.

The elf was ignoring the chaos, his hands shaking as he gripped the strange device. I could feel the elemental power moving from it into the crystals that adorned his hands and then into him. It was like a storage device that could hold the power of a thousand elves at once, and he directed it at the pillars.

I couldn't let him, so I tapped into the helmet I wore

and pulled the energy I needed from the crystals. Then I stepped closer. My air barrier butted against something he was controlling, the pressure making it harder to stay in control. It drew his attention.

"You can't stop me," he said. "Not when the great Kirdash aids me."

I frowned, wondering what he was talking about, but I wasn't going to stop.

"The great Kirdash isn't enough," I replied as I pulled my abilities together. Zephyr's mind was still melded with mine, and it boosted me as well.

I threw everything I had at taking away the elf's control, but nothing budged. Desperate to find something to aid me, I checked the helmet again. It was pouring energy into me as I fought the elf.

Boost the pillars instead, Zephyr suggested. *You need to drain him or the device he's holding.*

The idea was perfect, and I stopped pushing the elf and reached for the crystals housed in the center of each pillar. I was grateful that my reach was so great I didn't need to stand in the pillar forcefield, but I could feel the elf's connection.

They were fighting him, slowly draining him of power as they did. I had no idea how strong they were and how much energy they had left, but I connected with them and began refilling them.

It hurt since the pillars were not designed to be conduits in an elaborate tug of war or filled while they were using their power, but it worked. The pillars got stronger.

I had no idea how long I could keep it up, and I could

still hear the sounds of battle, Nuri, Roth, Sen, and Zephyr were keeping those in the portal room occupied and stopping them from getting to me. Any simple thing could sway this fight one way or the other.

As if he'd read my mind, I felt the slow, creeping presence of Kirdash. The activity in the pillar area became more erratic as his mind approached. I wasn't surprised when he latched on to me, but it made my next actions a thousand times harder.

Nuri turned back into a normal bird as he landed on my shoulder, feeling my need for his aid.

You can't stop me, the dark elf said.

Actually, I can, I replied, but I wasn't as confident as I sounded. *Could* I stop him?

Nuri began helping sever the connection, but I was still supporting and protecting the pillars.

Kirdash laughed, then his mind started moving through the area. The forcefield moved and shifted with him, his mind manipulating it through the portal.

Zephyr sent waves of calm to me despite the strain Kirdash put on our bonds. Before I could stop it, however, the earth pillar exploded. I gasped in pain as my connection to it was severed.

The elf near me chuckled and focused his attention on the three remaining pillars. Fear gripped my heart since it would now be easier for him to break the others.

I tried to move forward, but my air barrier met his again. It would drain more power from him to keep me out, but it was also draining my power.

Can we get more of our elves in here? I asked Zephyr.

The room was quieter, but I didn't know if that was because we were winning the fight.

I needed other powerful elves to join me.

Kirdash grew smugger and gripped me tighter. I had to decide. Did I defend my bonds with my mythicals from the pillar forcefield Kirdash was throwing at us, or did I protect the pillars from the elf trying to break them?

When Kirdash pulled on my bond with Nuri, I realized my answer. I was nothing without my mythicals.

Focusing on Nuri's instructions through the pain that flared as Kirdash tried to break my bond, I moved in from the side. Although I'd protected myself against the dark elf more than once this way and across the portal, I found it harder than ever to push him back.

Finally, I managed to break part of the connection, the pressure easing on my mind and bonds. Zephyr came closer. Sen bounded onto my other shoulder, joining the fight. I wasn't sure how much difference it would make, but I was grateful they were standing with me.

Before I could push Kirdash back farther, however, the fire pillar shattered, bits of rock and dirt flying at us. They bounced harmlessly off the air barrier but made it clear this needed to end soon, or it was going to be too late.

I doubled my focus on Kirdash. My mythicals worked with me to yank our minds and bonds out of his control. I found another thread of connection and attacked it, and the dark elf left our heads.

As always when he forced himself on our bonds, I felt gross and sullied, my mind violated. It distracted me, but I was aware that Kirdash wasn't gone and the elf was still trying to take out the pillars.

Pushing Kirdash back alone, I attacked anywhere I felt his mind. I also stepped closer to the elf, adding to the pressure and hoping I was hurting the elf as much as it hurt me. I focused on the two pillars, but the helmet was down to two crystals now, air and water.

Although the pillars were still fairly strong, their attacker was putting them under a lot of pressure. The pillars were liable to break, so I needed to protect the area the same way as the forcefield and the pillars.

A light bulb switched on. Instead of feeding the pillars' power into already-powerful crystals, I needed to merge my mind and control with the pillars and strengthen their forcefield and ability to protect themselves.

I could have kicked myself for not realizing that was the best way to keep them safe, but I couldn't waste any time. I felt for the pillars' control to figure out how they were protecting the area. Then, instead of fighting them, I merged with them. Zephyr still had his power melded with mine.

I felt the energy of the pillars, and I provided power to them. The elf grunted, shock and pain passing across his face. I was making a difference.

Grinning, I decided to push harder. We needed to stop or drain this elf.

No sooner had I thought this than his pressure on me and the air pillar grew. I fed the defense everything I had.

"Give up," I said, holding firm. "You can't defeat me. You'll run out of power first, even with that thing you're holding."

The elf didn't reply since he was under too much strain.

I wasn't sure I could do any better as the pressure on the pillars and our minds increased again.

Kirdash returned, but he didn't attack my mind and elements. Instead, he joined the attack coming from the elf. As I had merged with the pillars to make things easier on them, Kirdash merged with his soldier on this side of the portal.

Fury filled me as my head throbbed. I had been pushing so hard for so long that it was taxing my abilities. I could hold on longer, however, so I did. They had to provide the overwhelming force and keep pushing for another outcome. All I had to do was hang on.

There's help arriving. They just need to get to us, Zephyr said as he ran toward the front of the building. Shots were fired, but not in the portal room.

I'll get them here. Roth galloped in that direction. That left Sen and Nuri on my shoulders. I wasn't sure what they could do to help until Sen jumped down, pushing forward in my air barrier until she was up against the other elf's barrier.

I kept the pillars from taking control of her, which they would have done when she entered the field. Before I could stop her, she'd burrowed into the ground and wriggled under the elf's feet.

I held on, drawing more power from my helmet. She blasted his feet with ice, then hit him with a dart from her gun.

It distracted him from his task, and the pain lessened in my head. The elf looked down at Sen as she tried to insert another dart while moving around him.

Fear gripped my heart when he tried to stamp on her.

She wasn't as fast while she was burrowing through dirt. I could feel that she'd weakened the elf, his body fighting the sedative coursing through it, but that still didn't mean he was going to be easy to defeat.

I helped her move, taking control of the earth and getting it to part for her. She rolled around as he almost danced along with her. Now and then, she managed to hit him with her icy projectiles, but her next dart went wide.

Finally, he anticipated her move, and he slammed his foot down right where she popped up. His foot connected with her head, and I yelped from the pain that flared across our bond and from fear that he'd done something far worse to her.

The bond held, however. She tucked herself in a burrow, her pain fading but her enthusiasm gone.

Be careful, I told her, sending warm feelings her way.

A moment later, the air pillar exploded. Kirdash had hit it while I was distracted.

Another flare of pain filled my head, making me wince. There was only one pillar left, and if I didn't keep it safe, there would be nothing I could do to stop the dark elf from walking through and tearing this world apart.

We need help now, I told Zephyr, hoping the cavalry would arrive soon. *Only water left.*

I dug in, pulling on my water crystal and hoping it would be enough. Something needed to change. Almost drained and relying on the helmet I wore, I couldn't hang on much longer. If I couldn't keep this connection going, then no matter who arrived, they would be unable to help me defend the remaining pillar.

As Nuri flew closer to the elf, I realized the air bubble I

was holding around myself was no longer butting up against his. He had let go to focus on water, and as the white crystal on the glove on his hand grew dim, it retreated farther. I was sure that he wasn't using the element anymore.

I ran at the elf. Nuri swooped in front of his face and turned into a fireball as I hit him from behind. He stumbled forward but kept his grip on the elemental battery he was carrying.

My martial arts kicked in, and I used the air around me to speed up. In a few seconds, I was holding the dark object, and he was on the ground. He'd had no understanding of how to defend himself.

The pressure on the water pillar lessened as he lost focus, and I sighed in relief. This was better. The device in my hands connected to me a moment later, however, making my hands sting. I wasn't sure what it did or how it worked, but it tugged at my connections.

I put it down, but it fought that as well, latching onto me like Kirdash did.

Gritting my teeth, I resisted.

Go with it, Zephyr suggested. *You've got nothing to lose.*

The elf I'd knocked over got up and lifted his gloved fist, the water crystal on it shining. Zephyr was right; this fight wasn't over. I needed a miracle, or I was going to lose.

CHAPTER TWENTY-SIX

I gave in, letting the strange device connect with me and my elements. It sucked them greedily at first, which hurt, then stopped, almost severing the connection. It shook, heated up, and then reconnected.

Although I had hoped it could help, I tried to focus on the rest of my task. My mind was melded with the remaining pillar, and Kirdash and his soldier elf were still trying to break it.

When the elf drew on the water in his crystal, I hit him with an air blast to knock him away from the pillars. He blocked, but his crystal dimmed.

Suspecting air wasn't his element, I grabbed more, drawing on what remained of my air crystal.

The device finally opened up to me, but I was dismayed to find it was almost empty. Like the stone tablets, there was a pull to fill it again. It wasn't as bad as the tablets, but this device could do little to help me win this battle.

I tried to shut it down or put it down, but it didn't let go. Kirdash pushed again, so I continued to hold it and defended myself. A moment later, a fireball came my way. Thankfully, Nuri saw it and flew to intercept it, swallowing the fire as if it were nothing.

The elf continued to hurl the element. He was a fire elf and had plenty of his element in the tank. I tried to counter it and reach for control of the heat in the area, but it was one task too many. Kirdash took that opportunity to hit me again.

Zephyr and Roth rushed toward me. The pain flared in my head as the water crystal in my helmet ran out.

The pressure grew, and I had nothing to back me up and very little left in me. A mind merged with mine, then another. I glanced back to see Emily and Sierrathen. They stayed with me as I relaxed.

Kirdash and his soldier continued to push through our defenses, and my stomach twisted with hunger. The pillar was under so much strain it began to crack, its age and the constant pressure taking their toll.

I tried to hold it together, but it was too late. I was too drained to access another element, and I didn't have any other elementals connected with me to hold the pillar together with the physical earth element. Before I could call for an earth elemental, the pillar broke in half and the crystal spilled onto the floor.

The elf laughed, and the pressure went away. I dropped to my knees, my head swimming and hurting so much I felt sick. My mythicals gathered around me, Zephyr's hand going to my shoulder.

It was over. There was nothing to stop Kirdash from opening this portal. Three were open. Unlike the previous two, we couldn't bury this one under rubble. We had no way of making it harder for someone to come through. This portal was large, and it was going to stay open.

Zephyr helped me to my feet as Seth ran in with elves I recognized from the Sanctuary. It was too late, and their faces showed their disappointment, but this wasn't over.

I was still clutching the device, not sure how to get rid of it and switch it off. When more soldiers came in, they tranquilized the dark elf and dragged him away. I focused on the box.

Can you put it down? Zephyr asked for the third time, worried about me.

I shook my head. I tried to drop it, but it was as if someone had glued my hands to the side of it.

"What does it do?" Sierrathen asked as she came closer.

"It seems to store elemental energy. It's also doing something else. It...checked me out when I first picked it up."

Sierrathen's eyes widened, and she reached out. It connected with her too, and it warmed again before it let her go.

"Oh. I know what this is," she said. "It might not be useful right now, but that you have this and not the dark elf... Keep it safe, my dear."

I nodded, wondering if I needed to remind her I couldn't let go of it.

"What is it?" Zephyr asked.

"It harnesses not just the elemental energy but the energy and uniqueness of the bond between an elf and their mythical. It let go of me because I am unbonded. It is still connected to you because you are bonded. I believe you can sever your connection to it the same way an elf would sever their connection to a bonded mythical."

"Why would anyone do that?" I replied, although as soon as I finished speaking, I remembered I had considered it to keep mine safe. I didn't want to know how to do it, though.

"Well, most won't, and you don't want to sever your connection here. I'd say that having it bonded to you would be far better than anyone else. It does mean you can put it down and keep using it, however."

"But the elf couldn't. As soon as he dropped it, it stopped feeding him power."

"He had mostly drained it," Zephyr pointed out, shrugging.

Sierrathen looked thoughtful.

"It might be attracted to the most powerful elf nearby. I know the dark elf might feel that was necessary, but it could have been too drained to use while not physically connected."

"While that's interesting, I still can't put it down," I replied, my voice shrill.

"You should be able to. Try commanding it or whatever you normally do when you're communicating with your bonded mythicals."

Be snarky to it, Zephyr suggested.

I laughed out loud, and everyone else looked puzzled.

Sit, I tried instead as I moved to a nearby surface and tried to let go. Nothing happened, not even a wag of a tail.

Why won't you let me go? I thought at it. Surprisingly, it did that, falling to the floor at my feet.

For a few seconds, I stared at it. I didn't want to pick it

up, but I didn't want to leave it there. Zephyr grabbed the pack off my back, pulled out my snacks and handed them to me, then used it to scoop up the device.

Grateful his mind was working even if mine wasn't, I ate one of the packets of cookies and drank a bottle of fruit juice. It didn't help much since I had missed several meals, but it was better than nothing.

I had also missed some sleep, but there was nothing I could do about that now.

"We need to know how to construct more pillars," I said as more soldiers appeared, this time followed by the general. He looked around at the portal room with fear on his face.

With several of the others, I walked to the only pillar of the twelve that hadn't shattered.

"Get Minsheng and anyone from the Sanctuary who might be able to figure out how it functions to take a look at this," I said to Sierrathen. It was the first command I'd ever given her.

To my relief, she just looked at me.

"Aella?" the general called, drawing my attention to him.

He wasn't looking at me but at the portal. I could see why. Little white lines were appearing around the portal. Someone was opening it from the other end.

"Get every elf in here now, preferably fed and carrying every tablet, crystal, or energy-boosting device we've got," I said. "And then give every soldier a decent gun and plenty of ammo."

The general took one look at me and barked orders at the soldiers. Emily rushed off to get the rest of the elves. I strapped my bag on my back, felt around the cavern for the elements, and got a good grip on them.

Before long, elves, centaurs, and soldiers poured into the room. They formed a defensive line, earth elves and soldiers working together to move the earth and the barriers to provide cover and shielded areas to fight from.

"We're going to work as one," I told them. "Whatever comes through this portal in a moment, I want the elves to merge their elements with me. Everyone else, shoot anything or anyone that gets past us."

No one needed more in the way of a command. There wasn't time anyway. The portal was almost complete, and I was pretty sure something would come through from the other side in a moment.

I got into place, standing alongside my mythicals, as ready for a fight as I could be. I had drained my helmet, but someone had found fragments of an air tablet in the lab, and the centaurs assured me there were more reinforcements on the way.

When the portal flashed, completed and open, Dyneira trotted over and grabbed my hand. I barely had time to move to shelter before she pulled me into her mind palace.

Ronan joined us, along with Simon.

"Our portal is very active. I can't stay long," Simon said.

"Ours as well. It is still buried, but the earth elves are drained and can't hold it much longer," Ronan added.

"The Texas portal is open," I replied. No point in keeping it from them. "And I believe the dark elf is here at mine. Defend yours, but I think those are decoys. If need be, let them through but keep them from getting out of the rubble. Use lethal force if required."

"It's come to this? Do you wish us to send reinforcements your way?" Simon asked.

"It's too late. You can do nothing to aid us now. Hold your portals, and we'll do what we can here. I'll see if the general can send you soldiers to help, but you're on your own for now."

I nodded at Dyneira. I had the information I needed and did not want to waste more time.

"Good luck, Henera," Ronan said. "And remember, this is scary, but it is your destiny. You can defeat the dark elf and his forces."

I blinked at the encouragement.

"We made you for this fight," Simon added. "And you're not alone. We are with you. If not physically, then in spirit."

Dyneira switched off the connection, sending me back into my body. The centaur put her forehead against mine.

"I would not stand in battle beside anyone else. Whatever comes through that portal, be it the dark elf or his minions, I know you will fight. We will not let evil win. Not for long."

I exhaled, wanting to cry but also wanting to make the people with me proud.

Give them a speech, Zephyr said. *You're getting quite good at them.*

You know, you could give them a speech. I sighed and rolled my eyes, but I got back up and stood where everyone could see me.

It didn't take long to get everyone's attention, but it gave me a moment to think about how I could begin.

"I have fought with many of you before, but I know you are here for one reason: you care. You care about this planet. You care about the people on it. You care about the people near you. You care about being free.

"Together, we can make sure all of that is safe. No matter what comes through that portal, I will stand in this cavern between them and everything we care about. Will you stand with me?"

There was a roar of approval. A moment later, someone started chanting "Henera," and everyone joined in. It echoed around the cavern and made my heart beat faster.

I had to do what I'd promised.

No matter what, I'd stand in the way of whatever came through that portal.

CHAPTER TWENTY-SEVEN

I waited, trying to stay calm. Despite making a speech and everyone cheering, an enemy was coming, and we had no idea when.

As the minutes ticked by, I wondered if they had changed their mind and would attack through a different portal because I was here. Did they want to face me head-on?

They'll come for that box if it does what Sierrathen says, Zephyr remarked.

Even if they know I have it?

They don't know for sure that you have it, but they'll want it back.

I suspected Zephyr was right, but I didn't want to find out. Despite having faced battle, the dark elf, and his soldiers before, I was nervous and scared. We couldn't win every battle. The portal being open was evidence of that. Sometimes we lost.

Although good people backed me up, we were spread out across multiple locations, and we could only react.

Finally, there was movement; the portal rippled as a dark elf appeared. I didn't have to do anything with the air I held. Several soldiers opened fire and hit the elf with tranquilizer darts before she could take more than a couple of steps.

More appeared, coming through faster as they got going. Although the soldiers fired at them too, a few dark elves survived long enough to fight back.

Some of the dark elves were wearing the fancy armor we'd seen before. It was impervious to darts and bullets.

I helped guide the bullets and darts, aware I wasn't at full power. I didn't want to use up what elemental magic I had left doing something extravagant when simpler methods were more effective.

Although we'd lost soldiers in the earlier battles and some were wounded, they were giving everything in this battle and were allies I was glad to have.

The force of dark elves slowly grew, and with them came elemental magic. They built an air barrier around themselves, then started throwing fire.

I tried to wrestle control away from them while letting the others handle the fire. Several times Nuri flew across me, catching a fireball meant for me and swallowing it.

The battle started well, many of their number going down not to rise again or knocked back through the portal. I attempted to make the targets vulnerable but more came through, and it was harder to take down the ones wearing fancy armor.

More of our elementals were dragged into the fight until there were over a hundred elves slinging magic inside the cavern. It didn't take long for the area to start shaking.

Zephyr and I merged our control to brace the ceiling and walls, but the damage wasn't being done by another earth elemental. The battle was so fierce and so many people were moving inside the cavern that it was coming down.

We can't waste energy trying to fix it, Zephyr said. *We've got to let it fall without hurting anyone.*

I hesitated, not sure that was possible. Zephyr set his mind to work with where it was breaking and made sure the parts of the cavern ceiling that fell rolled outward and revealed the sky. It was fighting gravity, and it drained our earth and air abilities, but nowhere near as much as if I had repaired the building.

The light from outside startled our elves, centaurs, and soldiers, but it was distracting for the dark elves, who reacted with hesitation.

Taking advantage, I knocked some of them over with an air blast before aiding Zephyr. When I used air in battle, I sucked power from the tablets I carried, and when I used the other three, I used the helmet, aware that the crystals had only the power Sierrathen had refilled.

The dark elves kept coming. Although we were taking them out of action, they were relentless and, unlike us, hadn't already fought a battle.

The odds weren't in our favor. Not even close.

We fought on, not one person giving up.

As the dark elves erected yet another air barrier and pushed me back, I wondered if the enemy would kill us or capture us. They were relentless.

I took a deep breath, scanning the elementals with me. Most had run out of power. This was dire.

Not wanting to give up, I tried to think of another way to get past them. Not long after, the power in my helmet ran out in the earth crystal, and the air tablet fragments started to draw on me. Sen ran up and pulled them out of my hand.

For a second, I felt compelled to snatch them back and feed them, but the connection broke, and she tucked them into my bag. I focused on the problem again as Nuri swooped down and caught another fireball.

It didn't take me long to notice that Roth was one of the few mythicals who was not struggling. He was finding water so quickly and efficiently that the circlet on his forehead was pumping out a stream of water and he was practically flying as he hit his targets.

I grinned, wondering how he'd become so effective in battle until I noticed where he was. Roth was leaning against the broken water pillar, the crystal inside it pulsing with light.

I powered my way over to it and stuck my hand on it. It held a lot of raw energy.

It's giving everyone who can connect a boost, Roth told me.

"Water elementals to me," I called above the din, then looked for the major and Dyneira. They had instructed their teams to defend us at all costs. Soldiers and centaurs shifted to flank us, took out anyone targeting us, and aided water elves in coming our way.

We were hit a few times before Zephyr managed to help me erect a temporary air barrier in front of us. When I realized I was in danger of running out of power, Zephyr morphed into dragon form and landed in front of us.

Everything got harder. His mind no longer melded with

mine or worked with me to push them back. I shielded behind him for a few seconds and got my breath back, but they switched their focus to hitting the soldiers and centaurs with elemental attacks.

When another wave of dark elves arrived through the portal, we couldn't wait any longer. It was time to hit them with whatever this crystal would give us.

The water elves merged with me and connected to the crystal, huddling close. As we combined and the energy from the crystal powered into us, I moved to the front, and Roth came up beside me. The water near us was easy to find and pull on.

I grabbed whatever was nearest and sucked it out of the air and earth to start pooling it and feeding some into Roth. I also built a floating reservoir behind Zephyr. It grew quickly, the crystal so full of elemental energy it could have powered a factory for a week.

Now, I said to Zephyr. The area behind him was unable to hold any more water without it running the risk of drowning the elves creating it.

The large dragon leaped into the air, going through the large opening in the cavern roof and revealing us to the enemy. Roth and I started using the water. He hit single targets, driving them back, and I did the same. Emily stepped up to attack them too.

With them creating pincers, I grabbed most of the body of water and, with the help of the other water elementals and the crystal, lifted it and jetted it forward as hard as I could.

I was amazed at how well it worked. The dark elves were washed away. More air elves stepped up to sweep the attackers off their feet so I could hurl them back to the elven homeworld.

I kept pumping out water until it was gone and the cavern was soaked. We'd managed to push back over half the living dark elves and some of the dead and unconscious as well.

The fight went out of them, and I thought we had won the battle. I hastily helped the other elementals push back the last few dark elves. They also shot them with dart guns, and I did the same with my weapon.

More fell, and we advanced. I could feel the mood in the open cavern changing as we retook the ground despite our exhaustion. The crystal from the water pillar had turned the tide.

When there were only a dozen elves left, three of them wearing the special armor and throwing elemental bolts with precision, my blood ran cold. Kirdash's mind crept into the cavern.

At first he tried to hide his presence, but our minds kept touching, and I pushed him back. Connected to the crystal as I was, I felt as if I could handle him, but he was very powerful, and I didn't want to face him on this side of the portal.

Although he tried to latch onto me, I kept my mind out of reach, wanting to tire him. He'd have been pushing.

The elves around me came closer, many of them picking up on the dark elf's presence and joining their abilities with mine. We became one big network committed to protecting our world from the dark elf.

His mind came closer, and the disadvantage of so many being connected was that we were not as nimble. He found our group and quickly homed in on my presence among them.

As exhausted as I was, there was little I could do to stop him latching on and pushing into my head.

I have to hand it to you. You don't give up. But you should know when you're beaten.

And you should know when you are fighting for the wrong thing, I replied.

Nuri sent me a calming wave of energy, and I pushed myself to defend my mythicals and break the connection.

Unlike on previous occasions, the dark elf didn't seem to be trying to take my bonds. He explored them, getting into their heads and probing.

I think he's looking for a memory, Zephyr said.

Of what?

The device we have?

How do memories help? He made it and brought it here, didn't he?

Sierrathen implied that he found it.

If he didn't make it, then who did?

It wasn't a question for now, but it was the one my mind wanted to ask. Instead, I fought his control, pushing him back more easily than I'd have expected. I still connected to other elves, and while the centaurs and soldiers might have no idea what was going on, I had to protect them.

As he retreated, I followed him, constantly severing the connection to keep the world safe from his influence. I wasn't sure it was working until he disappeared, slipping back through the portal and leaving nothing behind. No dark elves were left standing, the soldiers and centaurs having taken care of them.

For a minute, no one moved. Everyone was waiting to see if this was a lull or more would come. Then I stepped forward, going to an armored elf I saw on the ground. I undid the straps and pulled it off. It pulsed with magical energy. I handed it to Seth, the nearest elf I thought it would fit.

He had a bruise down one arm, and he winced as he limped over. Many of the elves were the worse for wear, and we didn't have much more fight in us if another wave came.

"Let everyone who can rest," I said to him. "We'll keep an eye on the portal and figure out how to defend it if they give us the chance."

The young fire elf nodded and began ushering everyone away. I stayed where I was as soldiers, elves, and centaurs tidied up the space. My mythicals gathered around me, giving me their equivalent of a hug.

We'd won the battle, but as I looked at the open portal in the middle of the cavern, I suspected we were losing the war.

EPILOGUE

The device before me looked as innocuous as it had when I'd seen it lying on the ground. It wasn't, of course. It had bonded to me, and that was what my Shishou was trying to investigate.

During the last few days, we had spent an astronomical amount of time in the labs at the Texas portal site. The rest of the time, we ate, slept, and poured elemental energy into our storage devices. I carried one of those and tried to get it to respond.

Sierrathen thought this was very special, but if that was the case, it was awkward to use and little more than a battery.

Minsheng tapped buttons and monitored the object. It didn't fluctuate much, even when he had me pour energy in and pull it out.

I was about to suggest we give up for the day since I had to get back to patrolling the open portal site. Although they hadn't ventured through again and everything had been quiet at the other two portals, attacks could take place at any moment.

There were also meetings about defenses, where everyone should be stationed, and who should be in charge of what.

With so many people involved, it wasn't easy to find answers to some of those questions. So far, everyone had recognized the need to limit the number of places requiring protection.

We split our earth elves, a handful of soldiers, and backup mythicals between the buried portals with instructions to fortify them against invasion.

That left the Texas portal, where I and the rest of our defense army were currently living. It wasn't ideal. There weren't enough beds for everyone, and we'd spent a lot of time focusing on making it easier to defend a second time. It was improving with each passing day, however.

More soldiers had arrived, with more infrastructure and more resources.

The elves at the Sanctuary were hard at work, helping the refugees recover and learn how to defend themselves. The best minds from every race were working together to figure out how to close the portals and reinstate the pillars.

"Try again," Minsheng said as he tweaked something else.

I sighed but did as he asked, popping the device down on the bench. No sooner had I done so than there was a knock on the door.

"The general would like to see you, Aella," the major said. "Something about a phone call and news about how we got where we are."

Despite being puzzled by this cryptic summoning, I was bored and curious enough to go without hesitation.

"We'll test this later," Minsheng called after me.

Although I could hear the frustration in his voice, he understood. I hoped whatever they were calling me away for would help.

"What do you need?" I asked as I strolled into the general's office with my mythicals.

Sen and Nuri were on my shoulders, and Roth and Zephyr flanked me. We barely fit into the office. He turned his laptop around, got up, and came to our side of the desk.

The President was on the other end of the video call and had a grave expression on his face.

"What's happened?" I asked.

"We've received some intel from overseas. A...country we find relations less than ideal with appears to have a portal."

"That's not great but not unexpected. How did you find out, and what are they doing with it?

"Let me show you," the President replied as he clicked some buttons.

His face moved to the corner of the screen, and an image appeared. It looked as if someone had taken it from a distance with a telephoto lens. It showed a large open portal and someone who had come through it, accompanied by armored elves.

I could barely breathe. There was an unknown dark elf talking to the leaders of another country. An elf who had come through a portal and made contact with another country deliberately.

This was very bad.

"It gets worse," the President said as I gathered myself.

"How much worse?"

"We have found evidence that those who joined the refugee elves in their attack on the Texas portal and the people meeting this elf are connected," replied the President as the general handed me a copy of the image.

"They are?" I asked. I didn't like the sound of that.

"Yes. They've been radicalizing our males, especially our youth, against elves and mythicals. In the beginning we weren't worried about it, but we are now."

"What do you want me to do about it?"

"We want you to go to their portal and find out who they're talking to and if we need to put a stop to it. You're authorized to show them the footage from our portal and the fights we've had with the dark elves. Whatever is needed, and however you think is best."

It was a chilling statement, and it was telling me one thing.

Get that portal secure, no matter what you have to do.

I couldn't take my eyes off the guy in the photo. There was something about him that felt familiar. As if I'd met him, though I had not. He had purple eyes and a tall, strong body.

That's a dragon, Zephyr said. *Another dragon.*

PHOENIX SOULED

The story continues with *Phoenix Souled*, book 12 in the Dragon of Shadow and Air series.

Claim your copy today!

ACKNOWLEDGMENTS

This is one of those books where it's a little harder to thank people for how they were involved and how they helped. Not because people didn't help. They did. Lots of people are in my life in an amazing way and help me get the ideas in my head into something coherent and. So many people it's hard to thank them all. This book was easy to write but awful to second draft and lots of things went wrong in my life around the time I needed to.

I will always feel massive amounts of gratitude to LMBPN. The lovely people who polish my books, cover them, market them and generally keep me on track and take care of my writing journey make up a phenomenal team and I'm truly blessed.

All my amazing readers. I love hearing from you all and knowing who you love and who you love to hate. I adore all your messages.

To everyone who helped me finish the second draft of this book especially. Bryan and Bear you were both amazing when I came close to the last minute deadline.

ACKNOWLEDGMENTS

And to my tiny humans, who give me something to get up for each day, hold a piece of my heart each and show me that sometimes the most important thing in life is holding those you love close and making sure they know how much they matter.

Finally to God, who does the same for me when I feel broken and weary of the world's trials.

ABOUT THE AUTHOR

Jess was born in the quaint village of Woodbridge in the UK, has spent some of her childhood in the States and now resides near the beautiful Roman city of Bath. She lives with her husband, Phil, her two tiny humans (one boy and one girl) and her very dapsy cat, Pleaides.

During her still relatively short life Jess has displayed an innate curiosity for learning new things and has therefore studied many subjects, from maths and the sciences, to history and drama. Jess now works full time as a writer and mummy, incorporating many of the subjects she has an interest in within her plots and characters.

When she's not busy with work and keeping her tiny humans alive she can often be found with friends, playing with miniature characters, dice and pieces of paper covered in funny stats and notes about fictional adventures her figures have been on.

You can find out more about the author and her upcoming projects by joining her on facebook, by watching her live D&D streams, or emailing her via books@jessmountifield.co.uk. Jess loves hearing from a happy fan so please do get in touch!

Jess is also opening up her discord for fans to come chat about what she's up to, and see a few sneak peaks of future work. There's also a chance to become one of her beta readers. If you'd like to check that out you can do so here.

CONNECT WITH JESS

Connect with Jess Mountifield

Mailing list sign up
Facebook group.
Discord group
Actual play D&D stream: Twitch or Youtube
Email address: contact me here.

BOOKS BY JESS MOUNTIFIELD

Already published
Urban Fantasy
Dragon of Shadow and Air:
Air Bound

Shadow Sworn

Dragon Souled

Earth Bound

Night Sworn

Dryad Souled

Water Bound

Day Sworn

Pegasus Souled

Fire Bound

Light Sworn

Fantasy
Tales of Ethanar:
Wandering to Belong (Tale 1)

Innocent Hearts (Tale 2 & 3)

For Such a Time as This (Tale 4)

A Fire's Sacrifice (Tale 5)

Winter Series:
The Hope of Winter (Tale 6.05)
The Fire of Winter (Tale 6.1)

Guild of the Eternal Flame:
Wayfarer's Sanctuary
Protector's Secret
Healer's Oath

Other Fantasy:
The Initiate (under Holly Lujah)

Writing with Dawn Chapman:
Jessica's Challenge (#5 in the Puatera Online series)
Dahlia's Shadow (#6 in the Puatera Online series)
Lila's Revenge (#7 in the Puatera Online series)

Sci-Fi:
Fringe Colonies:
Alliance
Haven
Rebellion
Rebirth
Reclamation

Star Trail:

Hunted

Sherdan series:

Sherdan's Prophecy

Sherdan's Legacy

Sherdan's Country

Sherdan's Road (A short story in the anthology 'The End of the Road')

The Slave Who'd Never Been Kissed (A short in the charity anthology 'Imaginings')

New Beginnings

Santa's Little Space Pirate

In the multi-author Adamanta series:

Episode 1 – Adamanta

Episode 3 – Excelsior

Episode 8 – Phoenix

Episode 13 – New Contacts

Episode 17 – Sacrifice

Other:

Clues, Claws and Christmas

Non-Fic:

How to Write Lots, and Get Sh*t Done: the Art of Not Being a Flake

Find purchase links here

Coming soon:
Urban Fantasy:
Dragon of Shadow and Air:
Phoenix Souled

Fantasy
(Tales of Ethanar):
The Pursuit of Winter (#2 in the Winter series, Tale 6.2)

Books under Amelia Price
Mycroft Holmes Adventures:
The Hundred Year Wait
The Unexpected Coincidence
The Invisible Amateur
The Female Charm
The Reluctant Knight
The Ambitious Orphan
The Unconventional Honeymoon Gift
The Family Reunion
The Immortal Problem

Coming soon:

The Unremarkable Assistant

OTHER BOOKS FROM LMBPN PUBLISHING

Sign up for the LMBPN email list to be notified of new releases and special deals!

https://lmbpn.com/email/

For a complete list of books by LMBPN please visit:

https://lmbpn.com/books-by-lmbpn-publishing/

www.ingramcontent.com/pod-product-compliance
Lightning Source LLC
LaVergne TN
LVHW040614250326
834688LV00035B/550